SIGNAL 69: HOLDING JENNA

A BROKEN HERO PROTECTOR ROMANCE

THE SIGNAL SERIES
BOOK 4

LC TAYLOR

The place where light and dark begin to touch is where miracles arise.

—ROBERT A JOHNSON

CHAPTER 1

Jenna glanced around her classroom and smiled. While she loved every minute of what she did, she was ready for summer break. Two more weeks of school and she will have completed her second year at Clinton Middle School. She'd come to Clinton for a fresh start—a place where she could reinvent herself, or so she hoped.

At twenty-six, she never expected to be starting over. Yet here she was, alone and still feeling broken. Jenna absentmindedly fingered the scar hidden beneath her thick lock. It was the hidden reminder of how some people aren't who they say.

She'd met her ex-husband, Alec, during college. He was everything she thought she wanted, and after a short courting, they'd eloped during their senior year.

As an only child with both of her parents deceased, she never concerned herself with a big wedding. All that mattered to a young, barely twenty-one-year-old was marrying Alec. It was the only thing that mattered. Their marriage had been good for the first two years—but then, it took a turn she didn't see coming.

And the man she married became a monster.

At first, it was Alec's need to control her every move. He'd stripped her of her friends and any life outside of work. Looking back on things, Jenna realized it was so no one would know what was happening at home.

Alec would come home late from work, lose his temper, and take his anger out on her. Broken bones, stitches, and concussions all became a regular occurrence for her—that and the lies she told to hide the truth. Her co-workers thought she was the clumsiest woman ever. That or they suspected and were too embarrassed to find out what was happening. It was easier for them to stick their head in the sand than deal with her drama.

That was all before she turned twenty-three. The final straw was the night he nearly killed her. He accused her of having an affair with a fellow teacher at the school she'd only been teaching at for a year. He'd punched her hard, knocking her off her feet.

Jenna was too close to the top of the steps and tumbled down the stairs. Her head and the banister became intimately acquainted that night. Her finger traces the reminder as she recalls the event that changed her life.

Alec had no choice but to take her to the hospital since her head was split open like a busted-open watermelon. The ER immediately admitted her. Of course, she lied profusely about what happened, but a nurse stepped in and confronted her when he'd finally left to go to work. Jenna had been terrified, but something about the older woman made Jenna confess to what happened—not to mention the ongoing abuse. That day, a stranger saved her.

The doctor on duty called the police, who immediately arrested her husband. Six months later, she had her divorce, a protection order, and nowhere to go. After selling their house, she'd taken what little money she made from the sale and moved to Clinton. She kept to herself the first couple of months, but Becky, a fellow teacher, had been persistent and finally wore her down.

Becky became the best friend Jenna hadn't realized she needed. Not only that, Becky knew she'd come out of a pretty bad relationship, but she never pushed for details. Since Alec was rotting in jail and didn't know where she'd moved to, Jenna felt like her past was just that—a past.

Smiling, Jenna and the rest of her co-workers waved as the buses pulled out. Only seven days remained in the school year, and she was beyond excited. Now that she was settled into her new life, Jenna looked forward to relaxing on the sand.

"So, did you decide yet?" Becky probed as they headed back into the building.

"Yeah… Maybe we could rent a bungalow and hang out at the beach. I know it's just down the road, but there's something about being somewhere that's not home."

"Well, let me know. I'm down for some sun and sand any day. And a bungalow would be perfection… Who doesn't want to wake up and walk directly out onto the sand?"

Jenna smiled at her friend. "Perfect. I'll let you know what I find."

"Sweet, keep me up to date. Call me later, bestie." Becky bounced down the hallway towards her class.

Jenna wished she had her spirit, but the years of abuse had made her reserved. Becky was a flirt and had no problem getting male attention, while Jenna steered clear of men. She didn't trust them and wasn't sure if she ever would. Shutting down her computer, she grabbed the stack of math tests to take home and grade. They would be the last grades she'd enter into the computer before posting grades.

Jenna tossed the bag into her passenger seat and buckled up. She was exhausted from the day and was eager to get home and crawl into a warm bath. When she'd moved to the town, she'd lucked out and found a cute, three-bedroom ranch in her price range close to the school. While she didn't need that many bedrooms, the subdivision made her feel safe.

Pulling onto the roadway, Jenna contemplated stopping for some takeout. She hadn't been to the grocery store yet, so she wasn't sure what she had to fix at home. Making a last-minute decision, she headed towards the Chinese place down from the school. They had great spring rolls, and the way her stomach was already growling, she knew cereal wouldn't cut it.

She'd barely made it half a mile when she caught the blue lights in her rear-view mirror. *What the fuck?* She glanced down at the speedometer and double-checked her speed. Nope… she wasn't going over the speed limit. For the life of her, she couldn't fathom why she was being pulled. Agitated by how her evening was starting, she turned to the nearest parking lot and parked her car.

And if she thought it couldn't get any worse, Sergeant Finn Judson stepped out of the patrol car.

Fanfuckingtastic. She thought to herself.

He was gorgeous but the most arrogant man she'd ever encountered since moving here. And now, he was walking towards her car. Jenna clenched her eyes shut, willing herself to calm down. Finn didn't just irritate her—nope. Her fucking body went haywire when the man was near. Jenna had finally pushed him from her head after their one encounter—instead, *the kiss* they shared.

Forcing a smile, she lowered her window, preparing for his presence. She'd run out of the bar that night and avoided him… until now.

Jenna wasn't ready to get involved with a man then—or now.

No matter how *good* his lips felt.

CHAPTER 2

FINN SAT IN HIS PATROL CAR, WATCHING THE CARS GO BY. Being a sergeant on patrol gave him the freedom to do as he pleased. Scanning traffic, he watched as a red Honda CRV passed by. Doing a double take, he realized both taillight housings were completely shattered. He watched, confirming they were no longer working. Only the tiny rear light in the center of the back windshield warned cars behind her she was stopping.

"*Fuck.*" Finn muttered as he turned on his lights and pulled into traffic; so much for not doing anything. The driver, who appeared to be a woman, pulled into a parking lot just past the intersection.

Putting the car in park, he radioed his location and got out. Straightening his sunglasses, Finn moved slowly toward the vehicle. Pausing briefly to inspect the lights, he moved to the driver's window.

"Good afternoon, Sergeant Judson. Why'd you pull me over? I am pretty sure I wasn't speeding."

The unmistakable voice of Jenna Hardy filtered through the summer air—a sound that still affected him straight between his legs.

Finn met Jenna at Crimson's bar one night when he'd been out with the guys. She'd been with Becky Louis, a girl he'd gone to high school with back in the day. Jenna and he hadn't gotten off on the right foot—in fact, he remembered being called a pompous ass by her.

Of course, that might have been because of the kiss he'd laid on her lips. Lips that had been seared into his brain since. Jenna had run out of the bar like her ass was on fire…and avoided him ever since.

Finn adjusted himself discreetly and leaned down to peer into her window. "Afternoon, Ms. Hardy. Do you mind stepping out of the car for a moment?"

"What? Why?"

He held her gaze. "Ma'am. Please step out."

Her eyes flared with anger as she pushed open the door and stood beside him. "What's the meaning of this? I wasn't speeding." She folded her arms across her chest, drawing his eyes to her plump breasts. When his gaze landed on her lips, his body reacted to how she pushed her bottom lip out in a pout.

"Are you aware both taillights are busted?"

Shoving around him, Jenna groaned as she stormed toward the rear of her car. "That's not possible."

Finn pinched the bridge of his nose and sighed. Everything about this woman had him wanting to shake or fuck her—

neither was a good idea.

"What the fuck?" Jenna screeched.

Finn chuckled at hearing the dirty word escape her lips. It certainly wasn't something he expected out of her uptight personality. "Language, Ms. Hardy… but I assume your reaction means you weren't aware."

"Of course, I didn't know. They weren't broken this morning… I don't think." She pressed her hand to her head. "Fuck. I don't know. It's not like I check my taillights in the morning. How the hell could this have happened?"

Finn stepped behind her, inspecting the damage once more. "You didn't back into anything, did you?" He turned his head to look at her, catching a whiff of vanilla. Finn moved away, getting much-needed distance from her.

"Are you stupid? I would remember hitting something. What do you think I am, an idiot?" She pressed her hands to her hips and glared at him. Her anger was billowing off her in waves, which only made him chuckle.

Finn leaned toward her, a smirk covering his mouth. "Nope. But you can't drive this around."

"How am I supposed to get home?" Jenna threw her hands in the air.

Finn paused for a moment. "How about this? I'll follow you home, but you'll have to fix it before you drive it again."

Jenna blew out a frustrated breath. "Can you follow me to the dealership instead? I'll call Becky for a ride from there. Taking it home won't make any sense if I won't be able to drive it to get it fixed."

"Fine." Finn spun on his heel, leaving her standing there with her mouth gaped. He climbed into his patrol car and waited.

He watched as Jenna stomped back to her car and slammed the door. She pulled out of the parking lot in front of him and headed towards the dealership.

Finn couldn't help but think of the feisty girl in front of him. It'd been a long time since a woman had this much space in his head. After his marriage fell apart and Marley walked out on their life, he'd thrown himself into work. His parents were bitter over his divorce, constantly telling him he needed to beg her to come back. But Finn was done with her.

Marley broke everything he held sacred the day she revealed she'd been sleeping with her boss. He kicked her out and filed for divorce the next day. She tried to take him to the cleaners, but threatening to have her new boyfriend disbarred had stopped her in her tracks.

Finn had enough money that he wasn't worried about losing everything. It was just a matter of principle with him. Once she was gone, he'd sworn off women and love—aside from a few one-night stands, he didn't get close to anyone. At thirty-four, Finn didn't see falling in love any time soon. He wasn't sure he could trust someone enough to give his heart away—though as he thought it now, his heart thundered inside his chest as Jenna's car pulled into the parking lot and stopped. When she got out of the car, she was on her phone.

Finn saddled up beside her, his deep voice making her jump. "Driving while on the phone is against the law, Jenna."

He was stunned to silence when Jenna mumbled something before speeding up her steps and flipped him the middle finger.

He shook his head to hold back his laughter at the spitfire side he was finally seeing. He jogged to catch up to her. Finn glanced down at the phone in her hand. "You get a ride?"

"No. Becky isn't answering, so I'll call an Uber." She started fiddling with her phone again.

"Don't do that. I'll give you a ride. Go talk to them about your lights."

"I don't need your help."

"Jenna, stop being stubborn. Consider it my civic duty to take you home. Now go." He turned away from her to go back to his car. He needed to let dispatch know he would be tied up for a while. He'd barely released the mic when Jenna tapped on his window.

"Let me move my stuff. Unless you want to ride in back." He gave her a cocky grin.

"Not funny."

Jenna stood beside the passenger door as he cleared his stuff out and moved it into the back seat. He motioned for her to sit down, then shut the door. Jenna shoved her bag into her lap, and after giving him her address, she sat beside him, afraid to speak. She wasn't blind and knew some weird attraction was happening between them, but Jenna didn't want to acknowledge it.

When he pulled into the driveway, he stopped short. The remnants of her taillights littered her driveway.

"Well… guess that answers your question." Jenna jumped out before he had the car in park.

CHAPTER 3

Finn stared at the shards of red plastic in Jenna's driveway. It was apparent the shards of taillights had been crushed—both by whatever broke them and from her backing out over the tiny pieces.

"Jenna," Finn glanced at her, "Did someone hit your car last night?"

"No… I think I would have heard that, don't you?" She ran her hands through her hair and paused. "I mean…fuck. This is just great."

Finn stepped beside her and placed his hand on her shoulder. "I'll write up a report. That way, insurance will cover it for you."

Jenna glanced at him. She wondered what it would be like to have a man like Finn all to herself. He was so sure of himself, and damn—the man could kiss. Finn Judson was good-looking, no doubt about it. She shook her head and stepped back, putting the needed space between them.

"Thank you, Sergeant Judson. I need to go inside and make a few calls."

Finn pulled a card from his pocket and wrote his number on it. "Here, call me if you remember anything or learn something new. For now, I'll write it up as vandalism."

The sudden change in his kind demeanor confused her. Now Finn stood beside her, wearing his mask of arrogance.

Jenna snatched the card from his hands. "Thanks for the ride."

She stormed away and left him standing in her driveway. Finn watched Jenna as she closed herself behind her door. He wanted to scream at the woman.

He'd tried gaining Jenna's attention at the bar a few months ago. Jenna called him on his bullshit, saying she'd learned her lesson the hard way the first time and never intended to get tangled up with a self-serving, arrogant asshole again. He chuckled at the memory of her fire that night.

Getting back into his patrol car, Finn entered the information into his computer and pulled away from the curb. Soon after making himself available, calls piled up. Thoughts of Jenna were forced from his mind as he got into the swing of a busy evening.

━━━━━━

JENNA THREW her bag down on the counter. Her day had been going great—until *Finn* interrupted her tranquility. Getting pulled over and finding her car had been damaged was a headache she didn't see coming. Jenna racked her brain for any explanation of how her taillights might have gotten broken, but nothing stood out. Fishing her cell phone out, she tried Becky again.

"Hey, Lady." Becky chirped into the phone, "Did you find us an awesome summer hang-out spot?"

"I wish. I just got home."

"Wait…" Becky grunted. "It's almost six o'clock. Where the heck have you been?"

"Well, after getting pulled over by the police, I learned my taillights were busted out. Fortunately, I could get my car to the dealer for repair."

"Hold on… your taillights were busted? Did you get hit?"

"Nope. They were vandalized sometime last night, and I didn't notice this morning. Hence, the police stop."

"Shit. Did you get ticketed?"

"No. Sergeant Judson was kind enough to follow me to the dealer and bring me home. Which leads me to the reason I called."

Becky growled into the line. "Sexy Finn Judson gave you a lift?"

"Seriously, Becky? That's all you heard out of that conversation?" Jenna groaned at her friend's comment. "If *someone* had answered her phone earlier, getting in his car wouldn't have been necessary."

"Please… you can't sit there and tell me he's not hot as sin. A blind person could see that. And sorry I missed your call—I was tied up."

"Fine… focus, please. I need a ride tomorrow. I'm without my wheels until the lights are fixed."

"Sure… I can swing by in the morning and get you. Now, tell me about that hunk of a man in uniform."

Jenna sucked her teeth, sighing into the phone. "Nothing to tell. He's still arrogant and thinks the world revolves around him."

"Hold up, Jenna. I've known Finn since high school, and while I agree, he is cocky. He doesn't believe the world revolves around him. His attitude is his way of keeping people at bay. He married a horrific girl we went to school with, and she burned him."

"Wow, protective much?"

"Finn has helped my family and me in ways I could never repay him. And I, for one, would love to see him land a woman that appreciates him."

"Maybe you should date him then." Jenna laughed.

"No, thank you. We're only friends. Plus, I have my eyes set on someone else."

"Oh… do tell, Becky. I didn't know you were interested in someone. I always thought you'd be the perpetual heartbreaker."

"Nah… I don't want to jinx it… I like this guy too much to put it out there just yet. Plus—it's complicated."

"Fine, keep your secrets. Lord knows I have mine. Alright. I'll see you in the morning, bright and early. I'm going to take a hot bath, then peruse the internet for a rental on the beach. After today, I want a change of scenery."

"Alright, see you then."

Jenna disconnected and filled a glass with some wine. Since she never got the Chinese she wanted, she grabbed a bowl of cereal and sat at the high-top table in her kitchen. Jenna couldn't deny her attraction to Finn. She just wouldn't be telling Becky that anytime soon. Becky was right about one thing—Finn was a walking Greek god. His dirty blond hair and piercing green eyes made any heterosexual woman swoon. His hair was short except on the top, giving him a surfer look. And his body…*damn.*

But she was beginning to feel like a whole person, and a man would complicate her life. Something she was desperately trying to avoid. Dumping the bowl in the sink, she topped off her glass and locked it up.

Heading upstairs, she grabbed a towel. She was buried beneath the warm water and bubbles a few minutes later. Her body gave in to the soothing warmth, and her eyes became heavy. Not wanting to drown, she pulled herself out and toweled off.

Wrapping herself in a fluffy robe, she sat cross-legged on her bed, her hair wrapped precariously in a towel piled on her head. She opened her laptop and began scouring websites for a rental on the beach. Even though they lived in a coastal town, her house was six miles from the water. She wanted to wake up and stumble out the door into the sand.

Her eyes got heavy, and Jenna soon fell asleep with her laptop in her lap and hair still wrapped tight. Her dreams were filled with piercing green eyes.

CHAPTER 4

Finn sat behind the wheel of his patrol car, staring into the traffic. He'd found this hiding spot when he first joined the department. At the young age of twenty-one, Finn had thought he was slick. He'd worked hard and worked his way up the ranks within the department. By twenty-five, he'd become one of the youngest corporals in the department. He'd finished college to appease his parents, earning a bachelor's in criminal justice, but he knew, without a doubt, that being a police officer was all he wanted to do.

Shortly after graduating, he and Marley married. They'd been high school sweethearts. Finn thought she was his forever. For seven years, he'd devoted his life to her. Marley had been in his world other than work—they'd tried for children, but it'd never happened.

It wasn't until her affair was exposed that the truth came out. She'd had an IUD implanted to prevent any mishaps. Marley came from a wealthy family like him but claimed to understand his need to serve his community.

Marley had a business degree and immediately started working for a local attorney's office—which Finn supported completely. He wanted her to be happy and thought they were. Unfortunately, her career led to the demise of their marriage. Finn thought he'd given her the attention she craved—Hell, he'd doted on her every waking moment.

In the end, it hadn't been enough. Marley had been sleeping with her boss for five years. The day after hearing their marriage had been a lie, Finn filed for divorce. Marley tried to get money from him, but her infidelity had been her undoing. He'd left her with nothing. And there wasn't any part of him that felt bad.

All he'd wanted was a family until she ruined him. Now… that was something he steered clear of. Giving his heart to another woman was too much trouble.

He wondered about Jenna and what her story was. She acted like a frightened cat who hated men. Jenna moved here two years ago, and according to his friend, Becky, it wasn't until she wormed her way into Jenna's life. She steered clear of social gatherings and people. If he had to guess, she was running from a painful past like him.

He couldn't blame her if she were. Lord knows there were days he wanted to pick up and move, start fresh, away from his parents and this town. But he loved his job, which was enough to keep him rooted here.

Finn shook himself out of his visit down memory lane… memories he wished he could erase when a call came in for a fight. These were the moments he lived for. The adrenaline, the danger, the need to help those who couldn't help themselves kept him going. When Finn arrived on the scene, his patrol officers had it under control. He was happy to have strong men and women on his team because it made his job more manageable.

"Sarge," Hanson walked toward him, "you showed up at the party late."

"Seems that way. Everything under control?"

"Yeah—some out-of-towner made a pass at Harrison Lock's wife." Hanson shook his head.

"Fuck. Harrison didn't kill him, did he?"

"Nah—got some good licks in before the bartender broke it up. Harrison told the fucker to get lost or die."

"Shit. Where's this out-of-towner now?"

"Gone. The bartender said he hightailed it out when he told him the cops were on the way."

"Any idea where he went?"

"Nope, no name. Paid his tab in cash. Plus, Harrison said he doesn't want to press charges or anything. No damage here, so there is nothing for us to do. And I was hoping to get into a brawl."

Finn laughed, "You're an idiot, Hanson. Alright, I'll leave you to nothing then."

"Hey—some of the guys are going to grab a beer. Wanna come?"

"I think I'll pass this time. Don't drink too much. We still have work tomorrow—and it's not Friday yet."

"Getting old on us, Judson?"

Finn flipped his friend the bird as he walked towards his car. It was only Wednesday, for Christ's sake. His rotating schedule meant he had one more day than he'd enjoy his three days of freedom. His shift hours gave him time during the day with still enough time to manage a semi-normal sleep schedule.

Glancing at the clock, he saw it was a little after eleven. He decided to go to the station and wrap up paperwork for the night before going home.

CHAPTER 5

Jenna woke with a crick in her neck, the towel hanging loosely around her shoulders. Her laptop was lying on its side on the bed next to her. Stretching her head, she peeked at the clock.

"Shit."

Becky would be at her house in a little under an hour. Flinging herself off the bed, she dropped the towel and groaned when she saw her hair's mess. After brushing her teeth, Jenna grabbed a pair of black skinny jeans and a flowy tank top she covered with a short-sleeved jacket. Cuffing her jeans, she slipped on some sparkly sandals. Facing the mirror once again, Jenna stared at her reflection. Years of torment left her self-esteem somewhat fractured.

She knew she wasn't ugly, but seeing herself as beautiful… no, she didn't see that. At five feet, Jenna was petite, but she was not skinny.

Becky said she was curvy in all the right places—in other words, thick. She kept her naturally wavy hair long and usually wore it down, but today, it looked like a bird's nest, so she ran a brush through it and weaved her locks into a French braid.

Her once brilliant blue eyes stared back at her. They'd lost some of their luster when Alec nearly killed her. Jenna was putting on lip gloss when she heard the knock at her door. Rushing to grab her phone and bag, Jenna pulled the door open.

"What's up, Chicca." Becky smiled, "You ready to go?" Becky motioned towards her shiny red convertible parked in the driveway.

Jenna had teased her about her car, saying it was a midlife crisis, but it was beautiful, and Jenna was thrilled she'd agreed to pick her up.

"I know I gave you crap about your car, but it's gorgeous." Jenna smiled as she eased into the passenger seat. She was even happier she'd put her hair into a French braid since Becky rode with the top down. Jenna was just getting settled in when the dealership called her. It wasn't exactly the news she wanted to hear, but it wasn't as bad as it could have been.

"Dealership?" Becky asked.

She sighed as she shoved the device into her bag. "They said my car will be ready Friday afternoon. They have to order the housing for my lights."

"No worries, I can bring you home today and grab you tomorrow too."

"Thanks for doing this, Becks. You have been a great friend to me since moving here." Jenna smiled. "Swing through Starbucks, I'll treat you."

"You don't have to ask me twice." Becky made the detour, giving them ample time to get to work on time.

Jenna peeled herself from the car and headed inside with Becky. Waving as they went their separate ways, Jenna ducked into her class to get ready for her students. Teaching seventh-grade math was a passion she couldn't put into words. Seeing the kids' lightbulbs turn on when they got a concept filled her heart with joy.

Standing at her door when the bell rang, she greeted each kid with a smile. She felt good about herself for being able to teach these kids math, but she felt more pride in the connections she made with them as people. Jenna was confident that's why she had good math scores—because her students knew she cared, making them perform well.

The school day passed quickly. Since only six days remained in the school year, teaching had gone to the wayside, and they spent their time doing fun STEM activities. The kids enjoyed building things and making them work. It gave her time to grade the papers she'd forgotten about last night.

With the whole debacle surrounding her car, grading had slipped her mind. After the buses left, Jenna met Becky at her car. They passed the time chatting about a few spots Jenna had found on the beach and decided on a two-bedroom bungalow thirty minutes away. Becky was thrilled to be getting some beach time in. This was the first time she would take a vacation where someone wasn't dictating her every move.

As soon as Becky dropped her off, Jenna dropped her keys and bag in the doorway. Sifting through her mail, a letter caught her attention. It was from the department of corrections out of Hopewell. Jenna sucked in a sharp breath. One of the protection order conditions was that Alec could not contact her—even by letter. Surely this wasn't from him. Ripping the flap open, Jenna pulled the folded paper free.

DEAR MS. HARDY,

AS PER THE CONDITIONS OF YOUR PROTECTION ORDER, THE DEPARTMENT OF CORRECTIONS IS REQUIRED TO NOTIFY YOU OF THE EARLY RELEASE OF MR. ALEC BROWN. MR. BROWN DISPLAYED EXEMPLARY BEHAVIOR AND WAS GRANTED EARLY RELEASE PER HIS INCARCERATION CONDITIONS.

BECAUSE YOU WERE GRANTED A PERMANENT PROTECTION ORDER, MR. BROWN WAS REMINDED OF THE CONDITIONS UPON RELEASE. HE WILL BE REMANDED TO COMPLETE HIS SENTENCE IF HE VIOLATES THAT ORDER. IF YOU HAVE ANY CONCERNS OR QUESTIONS, YOU MAY CONTACT THE OFFICE AT 709-234-5678.

SINCERELY,

ALAN DANIELS

ASSISTANT DISTRICT ATTORNEY

Jenna crumpled the letter in her hand. Alec beat her within inches of her life, and he was getting out because of two years of good behavior. Her life had been irrevocably changed because of him. Moving like a zombie, Jenna collapsed into her bed, the tears she'd spent years expelling over that man spilled once more. Once she was done crying, Jenna set up her phone to wake her in the morning.

She didn't feel like eating, nor did she want to crawl out from under her covers. Instead, she cried again. This time, her tears didn't stop until she'd fallen asleep.

CHAPTER 6

BECKY ARRIVED AT HER HOUSE ALL TOO EARLY. JENNA DID her best to hide the deep purple circles under her eyes, but she wasn't fooling her.

"Alright, what the hell happened?"

"What… nothing. I didn't sleep well." Jenna smiled half-heartedly but could tell Becky wasn't buying her lame excuse.

"Bullshit. Jenna, tell me why you look like you've been crying all night."

Sighing, "Fine. I got some news I wasn't expecting, and I guess I got emotional about it. I'm fine, though."

"You want to talk about it?"

"No. I don't. So, can we drop it? Instead, let's talk about our staycation." And that's how Jenna changed the subject. They chatted about what they would do the rest of the way in once they got to the cottage. Jenna planned to spend as much time on the beach, soaking up as much of the sun as possible. Becky insisted they go out at night and live it up a little.

Once more, the day was moving at lightning speed, which was typical this close to the end of a school year. She was sitting behind her desk during planning when she was called to the office. Jenna laughed at a joke one of her co-workers made as she entered the main office. The secretary smiled when she pointed towards a large vase filled with two dozen roses. "Those are for you. They were just delivered."

"Oh. Who sent them?"

"Not sure. The kid who dropped them off said he was just the messenger. Maybe it says on the card."

Jenna picked up the beautiful arrangement and turned to leave. "Thanks."

"Arc you going to open the card?"

"Once I get back to my room." She smiled at the long-time receptionist as she hurried down the hallway. The flowers smelled divine. Setting them on an empty student desk, Jenna tugged the tiny card free. She had no clue who could have sent such an exquisite bouquet.

"Damn... Mrs. Reynolds wasn't kidding when she said they were big." Becky took a deep sniff, "And they smell nice. Well... who sent them?"

Jenna held up the card. "Was just about to find out." She palmed the card, carefully tearing open the sealed flap. Slipping the card out, Jenna sucked in a breath as she read the words printed in black on the cardstock.

Time changes nothing.

Becky was peering over her shoulder. "What the hell does that mean?"

"I don't know." Jenna's gut churned with worry. "Maybe it's a mistake. These must have been for someone else. Let me go up and ask Mrs. Reynolds where they came from."

Jenna practically ran to the front office, only to discover no forwarding address, but Mrs. Reynolds had ensured they were for her and not a mistake. Jenna grabbed the flowers and met Becky at her car.

Becky didn't pry. She didn't ask about the flowers again—instead, she spent the time begging Jenna to meet her for drinks after she was done at the dealership. Reluctantly, Jenna agreed.

Once she got home, Jenna grabbed a quick shower and blew out her hair. She grabbed a maxi dress from her closet, pairing it with her favorite heeled sandals. Once satisfied with her appearance, Jenna grabbed her things and headed out the door. She promised Becky she'd meet her at Crimson's at seven. After her long, weird week, Jenna figured a few drinks were just what she needed.

Pulling into the parking lot, the crowd slightly freaked out Jenna, but it was Friday, so many folks had the same idea for after-work drinks. Jenna took a deep breath and got out of her car. She was still not comfortable around a lot of men, but after some liquid courage, she'd try to enjoy herself. Worst-case scenario, she'd tell Becky she had a migraine and duck out. Locking her car, she texted her friend that she was there and pushed through the front door.

CHAPTER 7

Finn couldn't believe he'd been talked into meeting his squad off-duty at the bar. But here he sat, watching his friends and fellow officers drink themselves silly. He wasn't much of a drinker, barely drinking enough for a slight buzz. After sharing a pitcher of beer, he switched to water. Finn enjoyed watching them make asses out of themselves, and staying sober meant he could ensure they'd get home ok.

"Is that who I think it is?" Chase pointed towards a woman who'd just walked through the door.

Finn's breath caught in his throat. *Jenna.*

"Yep…that's Jenna Hardy. You know, Becky's friend. Which means—" Chase turned, scanning the bar, "Yep. There she is. Hey, Hanson," he called out to his friend, throwing darts. When Hanson turned to look, Chase cocked his head towards Becky. Hanson had a severe crush on the woman, but she'd told him repeatedly she wasn't interested. He didn't seem to take no for an answer, continuing to chase after her, anyway. The entire team thought it was funny to watch.

"I didn't know she could look so sexy." Hanson swallowed his beer. "I think I'll go invite them to our table."

"Sit down. You're drunk." Finn barked, making the whole table look at him, shocked at his outburst.

Chase grinned at his friend, "Whoa… Sarge has a crush."

"Fuck off, Chase. Hanson is three sheets to the wind. I don't want him to do something that would embarrass us."

"Alright, Sarge. I hear ya." Hanson held his hands up in surrender and sat back down.

Finn stood. "I'll be back. Going to take a leak. Don't let this asshole do something stupid." He made his way through the crowded bar, pushing through people on his way into the restroom.

Finn didn't understand why he felt jealous of Hanson, suggesting he invite Jenna to their table. He wasn't interested in her anymore. At least he was trying to convince himself he wasn't. Washing his hands, Finn took a deep breath and shoved out of the bathroom. As soon as he stepped into the hall, he collided with Jenna.

"Shit." He grabbed her shoulders, steadying her on her feet. "I didn't mean to run you over."

"I'm fine. Thanks." Jenna stepped out of his hold, and Finn felt her absence as soon as she pulled from his grasp. He stepped toward her, noticing her involuntary step back, causing her to flatten against the wall.

His hands came up to cage her against the barrier as he moved closer to her body. Finn stared at her, his mind racing as he tracked the movement of her throat when she swallowed.

"Fuck it." He mumbled as his head lowered and pressed his lips to hers.

Finn felt her body tense at first, but as he closed the gap between them and deepened the connection, she moaned, leaning into him. The kiss went on for what felt like an eternity, but the sounds of the bar broke through his lustful haze, and Finn tore his lips from hers.

Jenna looked equally shocked at what they'd just done. Her skin was tinted pink from the flush that covered her face, and her eyes were hooded as she pressed her fingers to her lips.

"That shouldn't have happened." She pushed under his arm and bolted, leaving Finn confused—not to mention painfully hard.

This was the second time she'd left him reeling after a fiery kiss. Closing his eyes and sucking the stale bar air into his lungs, he straightened from the wall, adjusting the not-so-small problem, threatening to bust out of his pants. Once he composed himself enough, Finn returned to the table and sat down.

"Damn, thought you might have fallen in or something," Grimes laughed.

Finn heard him, but his eyes were glued to Jenna, who was having an animated conversation with Becky. He could see Becky tense, her eyes cutting his direction, then shake her head and say something. Jenna's head bobbed as she leaned in and hugged her friend, then practically ran out of the bar.

"Oh…" Davis slapped his hand on the table, breaking Finn's gaze from Jenna. "You scared her off, didn't you?"

Finn growled at Davis. "No."

"Right. That's why she's leaving, and you can't seem to take your eyes off her." Davis held Finn's glare. "Why don't you just ask her out?"

"I did, remember? She called me a pompous ass."

"Knows you already." Davis drank the last of his beer. "I'm ready to go. See you in a few days, Sarge."

Finn narrowed his eyes at Davis. "Hey… you ok to drive?"

"No. I called an Uber. I might be a goofball, but I'm not a fuckup sarge."

"Good." Finn tapped the table. "See you on shift."

Finn sat at the table for a few more minutes before settling his tab and leaving. This kiss affected him just like the one he'd experienced with her before—hell, his dick got hard just thinking about both times he's tasted her soft lips.

But she *ran*… twice.

Her demons were strong, and Finn didn't need that kind of drama in his life. He didn't do messy, only quick and simple. Something told him getting with her wouldn't be either of those things—which meant he needed to steer clear. Cranking his truck, he pulled out and headed toward his house. It was the one thing he didn't get rid of after the divorce since it was his before they married. He'd picked it out because it was the house you bought for a family—something he wouldn't have now. Yet, he couldn't bring himself to sell it. As he approached his front door, he could hear the telltale sign of

Eros, his K-9 kid, waiting on the other side. Opening the door, he was greeted with dog slobber and kisses.

"Down, Eros."

Finn pushed him back and scratched behind his ear. He'd bought Eros the year before his divorce. After giving up on having kids, he convinced Marley to buy a dog. She'd sworn she was okay with getting him, but it didn't take a rocket scientist to know she'd appeased him.

Eros was the son of a God and was tasked with making people fall in love. Finn picked his name as a sentiment of his love for Marley. The funny thing was their failing marriage was the only thing it had cemented. But Finn didn't blame the dog for Marley's betrayal. Besides, Eros loved him unconditionally and was more loyal than any human could ever be.

After feeding and walking him, Finn headed inside and locked up. He found his thoughts straying toward Jenna again. Even though he knew she was fighting an inner turmoil, the intelligent thing to do was stay away from her—he wasn't sure if he could.

Her kiss had been imprinted on his brain… and was slowly seeping into his blood.

CHAPTER 8

Jenna locked herself inside her house after bolting from the bar. Finn's kiss had sent her into a tailspin that no one needed to see. Pacing her hallway, she ran her hands through her hair and huffed. She couldn't get involved with him—it was a mistake of epic proportions.

He was arrogant and domineering… two traits that freaked her out. Striping her clothes, she wandered into the bathroom and turned on the shower, needing to wash the tingling sensation he left behind off her skin.

The room filled with steam, and Jenna stepped into the stall, letting the scalding water cover her. The tiny pins pricking her skin washed over her as she braced her hands against the wall to calm her breathing. She was on the verge of having a full-blown panic attack. Grabbing the soap, Jenna scrubbed her skin, trying to wash away her fear.

This time, the fear was different—the desire she was feeling terrified her. Finn had caged her against the wall, and initially, her throat closed in panic. But as he pressed his body against her, then covered her mouth with his… Jenna realized she wanted him. She'd felt a molten hot desire for the second time, and Finn was the cause.

And that scared the shit out of her. She stayed under the water, scrubbing her skin until it was covered in red welts, the warmth of the water disappearing as she let her tears mingle with the falling water. Her therapist had warned her that specific triggers would incite panic attacks. She just hadn't expected it to be from lust. Because despite her fear, Jenna wanted Finn.

Her body tingled in ways she'd thought were buried all because of the sexy police officer. When the water turned to ice, Jenna finally stepped out. She wrapped a towel around her and stood at the sink, staring at her reflection.

Was this what she was destined to be?

A woman afraid of a man's touch, even when the touch made her body light with fire, not fear? Jenna stepped into the cool air of her bedroom, her flesh pebbling with goosebumps. Slipping on shorts and a tank top, she toweled off her hair and sat on the edge of her bed. She didn't want to be this person. One meant to be alone forever. It was barely ten o'clock, and she was hiding at home. She hightailed it out of the bar because she was too ashamed to face Finn. Standing, Jenna stretched her arms.

She needed wine.

Once in the kitchen, she grabbed a wine glass and filled it to the rim. She headed towards the living room, grabbed a blanket, and curled on the sofa. Scrolling through her phone, she opened her Kindle app and selected a romance book. Jenna just needed to disappear for a bit. With her glass of wine in hand, Jenna cozied up with her book boyfriend for the night.

FINN COULDN'T GET Jenna's expression of fear out of his head as she fled the bar. Even after a good night's sleep, he woke feeling like he needed to check on her. He threw on some sweats and decided to drive over to her house to ensure she was okay. He didn't want their kiss to leave her feeling guilty or afraid.

Finn pulled into her driveway, noting her car sat oddly in the driveway. The hairs on his neck tingled with concern, his cop senses on alert. He eased out of his charger and walked around her vehicle. Immediately, he saw the issue. Both of her passenger-side tires were flat. Running his hand along the front passenger wheel, he found the cause. A single slit, only two inches wide, was hidden inside the tire well. Quickly checking the rear tire, he wasn't surprised to find an identical cut. Someone had slashed her tires.

But why?

Finn stood, scanning the area for signs of people out and about. It was nearing nine in the morning, and if he had to guess, it had happened overnight. He couldn't figure out why someone would do this to her. He wiped his hands on the material covering his thighs before knocking on her door. His intentions for coming here seemed irrelevant now. Instead, he needed to tell her about the tires and call it into the station.

"Finn?" Jenna wiped the sleep from her eyes. He'd just woke her. "What are you doing here?"

"Well, I came to check on you. You left in such a rush last night after our kiss that I was worried I'd pressured you and put a look of fear on your face."

"Oh… um. I'm good." She shifted from foot to foot, obviously uncomfortable with his presence.

"Look, I hate to be the bearer of bad news." He stepped to the side and pointed toward her SUV, "But it looks like someone slashed your tires overnight."

Her eyes widened. "Please tell me you're joking."

"No. Come see for yourself."

CHAPTER 9

Jenna burst past him, praying he was messing with her. But she knew from his expression he wasn't. She didn't have to check anything when she got to the passenger side of her car. Both tires were as flat as they could be.

"I can't fucking believe this!!" Jenna was pissed. "Who the hell keeps doing this?"

Finn met her at the side of her car. He palmed the back of his neck. "I don't know, but I called for a unit to come by. You need to make a report of this, Jenna."

It was then that Finn took notice of what Jenna was wearing. She had on the tiniest pair of boy shorts he'd ever seen. They were molded around her luscious ass and the tank top—*fuck*. It was tight and did nothing to hide her body from his eyes. His cock immediately responded, threatening to tent his joggers like a teenage boy. As if Jenna could sense what was going through his head, she covered her chest with her arms. Unfortunately, all it did was press her plump tits together.

"Damn it. I need to throw on something before your co-worker gets here." She ran around him, darting up the steps before he could say anything.

Finn was glad his sweats were loose because his semi was hidden beneath the material, saving him from embarrassment. He pressed into his cock, trying to adjust himself as a patrol unit pulled up.

"Sergeant Judson, I didn't realize you were the complainant." The patrol officer greeted him.

"I'm not. Jenna Hardy is the vehicle's owner. I stopped by to see her and found both tires slashed."

"Oh."

The officer's clipped response told him he'd hear about this later—the gossip would burn through the department like wildfire. Jenna emerged from the house just as he was about to tell the rookie officer his concerns.

She'd changed, but it did nothing to quell his attraction or cover her up. Now, instead of the shorts, Jenna was wearing athletic leggings. They looked painted on, making him picture her legs wrapped around his waist. He watched as she spoke to the officer, his pulse thumping like a steady drum in his ears. He had this crazy urge to wrap her in his arms and protect her.

"See you around, Sergeant." The officer shook Finn's hand and left. He studied Jenna, hating that she looked utterly defeated.

"Hey," he pressed his hand against her shoulder. His actions did not elicit the reaction he was expecting. Jenna covered her face and burst into tears. Without thinking, Finn tugged her into his arms and held her while she sobbed.

"It's not that bad. Let's get you some shoes, and I'll take you to get some new tires. I can call a buddy and have it towed to the shop." He guided her towards the front door, helping her up the stairs. Jenna slipped on her shoes, grabbed her purse, and followed Finn to his car.

Jenna hadn't noticed he wasn't in his patrol car until she focused on his personal vehicle, which was just as sexy as him. "Wow, nice car."

"Thanks." His grin nearly melted all her worries—and panties, on the spot.

Jenna shook off the unwanted tingles of desire just as he pulled open the door and helped her in. He glanced over at her when he dropped into the driver's seat. She tried not to cry, but the tears rolled down her face in droves. Finn reached across the console and thumbed a teardrop off her cheek. "It will be alright, Jenna."

Jenna wiped her eyes. "Thank you, Finn. I don't know why you're helping me. I haven't exactly been nice to you."

"What are you talking about?"

"I'm pretty sure you remember me calling you a pompous ass the first time we met. And then running out on you after our kiss—twice." Jenna laughed softly, her smile making his chest constrict.

"That's not the encounter I remember, Jenna. And I'd say we're friends. Plus, being a civil servant, it's my duty to help a beautiful damsel in distress. Now, let's get your car straightened out."

"You didn't have to do this. I could have called Becky. She would have driven me."

"Nonsense. I was here. Plus, it lets me spend time with you."

"And I get to ride in this panty-melting car of yours." Jenna winked at him.

Finn tried to relax, shifting uncomfortably in his seat. He couldn't resist, so he teased her a little. "Are your panties melted?" His dick was ready to rip through his boxers.

"I'm sure if I wore any, they would be." Jenna realized what she said and covered her face, "Oh my god. That was so inappropriate. The stress is making me say stupid things." Jenna turned to look at Finn, his eyes hooded with lust.

She blushed and turned to look out the window, wishing she could climb out of it. Neither spoke again until they arrived at the tire shop.

"I'll be in to meet you in just a sec." Finn did not want to walk around sporting wood.

"You don't have to stay. I'll call Becky."

"No… It's not that." Finn rested his head on the steering wheel. "I can't get out just yet." He turned his head, glancing at Jenna and then at his tented pants.

"Oh." Jenna turned, pushing the door open, "I'll see you inside me… I mean, I'll do you… *Fuck*."

She darted from the car, slamming the door shut. Finn chuckled as he watched her rush inside the store. He willed his cock to settle down so he could get out and help her. Being around Jenna and not having an erection was proving nearly impossible. The sexual tension was thick, and now so was his dick.

CHAPTER 10

Finn didn't mention the word vomit she'd embarrassed herself with when she caught sight of his massive hard-on as they climbed back into his car.

"Thank you for helping me today. It was nice of your friend to tow my car at no charge. I could have paid him."

"It's no biggie. He owed me a favor."

Finn wasn't about to tell her he'd paid the two-hundred-dollar bill. He figured she'd be pissed and demand to pay him back. He suspected she did not know he had more money than he knew what to do with—although he only dipped into his trust fund for emergencies. The only things he'd used his trust fund for that weren't urgent were his house and car. The rest of his possessions were bought with his hard-earned money.

Until *today*.

He'd paid the tow bill, and then when she stepped out to call Becky, he had the manager put the best tires on her car. He told them he'd cover the difference and to tell her they were running a two-for-one special. Sitting outside her house, he was trying to find a reason not to leave.

"I can't thank you enough, Finn. No one has ever helped me out like this. I owe you."

"How about coming to dinner with me?"

She tensed, and Finn realized the idea scared her. So, he quickly added, "As friends."

"Friends?" She cocked her head. "I don't think that's a good idea. I appreciate your help today, but I am not in the place for this." She waggled her finger between them.

"You're saying you don't want more friends?"

"You know as well as I do. *Just* friends would be impossible between us."

Finn was disappointed, but he didn't push. "Well, when you're ready, you owe me dinner."

"I can just pay you or something."

"I don't want your money, Jenna. You need to realize some people like to help others without wanting something in return. And if dinner makes you uncomfortable, forget it."

"I'm sorry. I just haven't had the greatest experience with men. It's hard for me to trust there aren't ulterior motives."

Finn grunted. "You've obviously been with the wrong men."

"You have no idea," Jenna muttered as she exited the car. "Thanks. I'll see you around."

She shut the door with that, leaving Finn to watch her disappear inside. Someone had hurt this woman, and he didn't like that thought one bit. Finn pulled off her street, reluctant to do so, but he wanted to respect the distance she claimed she needed.

JENNA POURED herself some juice while she waited for Becky. She couldn't believe someone had vandalized her car twice and refused to let herself know it was her ex. Jenna got along with all her neighbors. She had a good relationship with all her students and didn't think any of them could do this. Which only left—

Becky's horn startled her, causing her to spill her drink. She quickly wiped up the mess and ran out to greet her friend. Jenna had showered and changed earlier, wearing a pair of fringed cut-off shorts and a tank with thin straps. Glancing at the downed roof, she pulled her hair into a ponytail and climbed in.

"Thanks for this, Becky."

"I wasn't doing anything, anyway. But can we talk about how your car has been vandalized twice now? It's freaking me out."

"It's pissing me off. I think I'll buy one of those video door-bell things. Then maybe I'll be able to catch whoever is doing this."

"That's a great idea. We can stop by the store and get you one. I'll come back over with more wine, and we can make it a girls' night in."

"Sounds good to me."

"Plus… we can talk about why Finn was here this morning. *And* why he left almost immediately after you last night." Becky waggled her eyebrows.

"Nothing is going on. He just came by because he thought he upset me at the bar. He wanted to make sure I was good."

"What happened that would make him think that? I don't recall seeing you two even talking."

Jenna blushed. "We ran into each other near the bathroom."

"Ok…" Becky looked at Jenna, confused. "Oh MY GOD. You ran out right after. What the hell did he say? I swear I would punch him in the dick if he were an asshole."

"He wasn't. I… he…" Jenna swallowed, the memory of how his lips pressed against hers felt.

"Umm… I see." Becky chuckled.

Jenna shrugged, not wanting to talk about it. "Can we change the subject?"

"Sure, for now. But tonight—I'll get your secrets. Wine is the world's truth serum."

Jenna couldn't help but laugh. She and Becky chatted about their staycation and how they were sad the year was nearly done at school. Jenna retrieved her car after a brief stop to pick up her new video doorbell. She was shocked to learn they'd put four new tires on for her. The manager told her they were two-for-one and replacing them all was best. She thanked him and paid her bill. Becky promised to be there at six so they'd have enough daylight to install the new doorbell. Jenna waved her off and headed towards the grocery store.

CHAPTER 11

Finn felt her before he saw her. He was standing by the steaks, trying to decide what to eat for dinner. She was bent over, hoisting a case of water into her cart, and hadn't noticed him staring. She was in a pair of jean shorts that were frayed around the edge, showing off just enough of her luscious bottom. Her loose tank top had inched up her back, revealing the smooth skin beneath it. Finn took two strides toward her as if on autopilot and stopped beside her cart.

His voice cracked when he spoke. "Jenna."

"Oh." she stood up fast, nearly knocking the cart into him. "Finn. How are you?"

He couldn't stop himself as he grabbed her neck and pulled her lips to his. He applied slight pressure, licking the seam and urging her to open. When she did, Finn groaned into her mouth. He became desperate with need. Jenna's hand pressed against his chest, fisting his t-shirt. A cough beside him caused him to step back.

"Sorry." He glanced at the older woman, smirking at their display, and smiled. Finn looked back at Jenna. Her lips were swollen, and her eyes were wide with disbelief. The flush of her skin made her even sexier, causing a growl in his throat.

She stiffened, glancing at the few people who were standing around gaping. "I gotta go."

She grabbed her cart and bolted. Leaving Finn standing in the middle of the aisle. Realizing he needed to say something, he left his basket on the ground and ran after her.

"Wait," he grabbed her arm. "Jenna. *Please.*"

She stopped, looking at the ground and refusing to make eye contact. "Finn. I don't know what's going on. But I told you... I'm not in a place to do this—with anyone. Now, please let me go. I need to get home. It would be best if you didn't come around me anymore."

She yanked her arm out of his grasp and hurried to the register. He didn't understand her reluctance to give this thing between them a chance. He wasn't asking for marriage... he just wanted to spend time with her. Finn'd never had to work this hard for a female's attention—but that only made her more desirable. Most of the women around here knew he came from money, and the ones who didn't, well, his uniform was a beacon to the rest.

But not her. She fought the attraction hard.

Jenna wanted him. He could tell by the way her body responded when he was close. Still, there was a barrier the size of the Great Wall of China around her. Defeated, he decided he needed to avoid her as best he could. Opening his phone, he called one of his buddies. He'd pick up a woman—

maybe a quick roll in the sheets with a willing participant would get Jenna out of his head.

"ALRIGHT, SPILL." Becky grabbed the bottle and poured another glass.

"What? There's nothing to tell."

"Bullshit. You've been snippy and slamming things around since I got here."

"Fine. I ran into Finn at the grocery store."

"And... don't make me hold the wine hostage, just tell me already. You still haven't told me what happened at the bar. I didn't forget about that either."

Jenna buried her face in her hands. "He kissed me."

"Where, the bar?"

Jenna groaned and mumbled, peaking at her friend through her fingers. "And the grocery store."

"Holy balls... I'd give my left tit to have the man I lusted after kissing me. Were they bad? Because that's the only reason I would run."

"That's the problem. They were fucking amazing. But I won't do a relationship again. The last one... well, let's say it was awful."

"Jenna," Becky placed her hand on her knee, "You can't let one bad relationship dictate all future ones."

"You don't understand. It wasn't just a bad relationship, Becky—."

"You're right." Her friend cut her off, her tone a bit put out. "I don't understand. But that's because you're guarded and won't share your past. A past I can tell was obviously a bad one. And I haven't pushed, but if you want me to understand why you're tucking tail and running from a man who is obviously into you, you'll have to open up to me. I consider you my best friend. I think you feel the same—so you can trust me with your secrets."

Jenna closed her eyes and sat up. Becky was right... she needed to trust someone with what happened, and since she felt the same about Becky, it was time to tell her what brought her to Clinton.

She spent the next hour telling the story she'd spent the last two years running from, leaving no detail out. If she were going to let someone in on her ugly past, she wouldn't sugar-coat it. When she spoke her last sentence, a weight she hadn't realized she'd been carrying seemed to lift.

"Fuck, Jenna. I can't believe you lived through that. I see why you're so cautious of people, men especially. But let me say this," Becky topped their glasses. "Finn is not Alec. I've known him for a long time, and the only thing that man ever wanted was a family. When his ex-wife cheated on him, she broke something in him. He's a good man who needs a good woman to show him love is real."

"I'm just not ready, Becky. I don't know if I'll ever be—even if my body thinks I am, my brain is all tangled up."

"Alright. I'll let it go. But think about it, will you? You could push away someone you deserve, not to mention he might be just what you need."

They spent the next couple of hours laughing and talking about their students. They had so many stories neither woman realized how late it had gotten or how much wine they'd drunk. Jenna could barely stand as she wobbled on her feet. "Sleep here or go to the guest room."

"No… I'm just gonna lay here… I'm too drunk to move." Becky mumbled, pulling the blanket off the back of the couch to cover herself.

Jenna waved her hands in the air, "Fine… Fine…" Almost tripping as she tried navigating up the steps. She fell through her door and face-planted on her bed, sleep claiming her almost instantly. Wine was a great sleep aid, especially when you empty two bottles.

CHAPTER 12

Jenna woke Sunday with the worst hangover imaginable. She forced herself to get out of bed and check on Becky, who was, as she vaguely remembered, passed out on her couch. After brushing her teeth, Jenna padded slowly downstairs and into the kitchen, then tiptoed into the living room. Becky, who was out cold on the sofa, had one arm over her eyes, the other dangling off the side as soft snores filled the room. Jenna couldn't contain the laugh when she saw her legs splayed over the edge.

"Becky," Jenna whispered, trying to stir her friend into the land of the living.

"Please don't speak." Becky groaned, her voice gruff.

"I made coffee."

"Thank God. How much did we drink last night?" Becky lifted her arm, allowing the light to hit her face. "Why must there be light… my head feels like a dump truck ran over it, backed up, and ran over it again to make sure it hit it properly." Glancing around the room, Jenna counted three empty bottles.

"Shit… I thought we only had two. But looking now, I see we drank three bottles. Our hangovers are well earned."

"Shit—what time is it?"

"Almost eleven, why?"

"I'm supposed to meet David at the school. He needed me to help set up something for field day tomorrow." Becky peeled herself off the sofa and searched for her shoes. "Can I get a coffee to go?"

"Why are you meeting Mr. Harlow on a Sunday?" She raised an eyebrow in question.

"He asked. I said yes." Becky didn't elaborate, but Jenna sensed there was more to her reasoning for saying yes.

Jenna smiled as she handed over a steaming cup of coffee. "Call me later?"

"Yeah… let me know if there is any other funny business around here. Hopefully, the new doorbell will deter any more shit from getting broken."

"I hope so. Thanks for hanging out with me."

Becky grabbed Jenna's hand. "And remember what I said. Don't let what happened keep you from something or someone good."

"Yeah, yeah. Have fun at work on a Sunday." Jenna locked the door behind her friend. Her head was still thumping like a bass drum, so Jenna decided the best action plan was to go back to bed.

She climbed under the covers and curled up under the covers. She closed her eyes and prayed the wine would work out of her bloodstream and take the splitting headache with it.

When she finally peeled her eyes open again, the clock on her nightstand read six p.m. She'd slept the entire day away, wasting a perfect Sunday. Getting up, she wandered downstairs in search of food. If the growling of her stomach was any indicator, she was starving. While shoveling cereal into her mouth, she noticed a notification on her cell phone from the doorbell app. Clicking on the alert, she opened a recording time-stamped that afternoon.

Finn had come by her house. He knocked on the door, then pressed her doorbell button. Smiling into the camera, he waved and waited. When it was apparent Jenna wouldn't answer, he looked at the door and then at the camera again. His expression made Jenna's heart hurt—he thought she was intentionally ignoring him.

She didn't want him to think she was that callous. She wouldn't have refused to open the door even if she told him to stay away. Clicking off the app, Jenna pulled up her contacts. Hovering over his number, she debated whether texting him would give him the wrong idea. After a moment of hesitation, Jenna fired off a few words of apology.

> Hey Finn. It's Jenna. I just saw you came by.
> Becky and I drank too much last night, so I
> slept through the doorbell and didn't hear it.
> I wasn't ignoring you.

> Thanks for telling me.

Jenna didn't know how to take his short reply. Did he think she was lying to him?

I'm not kidding. It feels like a herd of
elephants is still sitting on my head. Three
bottles are too many.

Jenna waited. She didn't owe him an explanation, but his being mad at her didn't sit well.

Three bottles?

Yeah. Stupid, I know. But we installed the
new doorbell and then got to talking. Didn't
realize we'd downed that many.

Hope you feel better.

Me too... work will suck tomorrow if not.
The last week of school is always rough.
Need to be ready for anything.

Are you?

Am I what?

Ready for anything.

Jenna smiled down at her phone. She was pretty sure he was flirting with her, and as stupid as it was, she was enjoying it. Texting was safe for her—it made her feel in control. Cocking an eyebrow, Jenna had a little fun with their banter.

I'm always ready...

You sure about that?

Let me check... yep.

What did you check??

If I was ready or not.

. . .

Finn?

Yeah…

I'm feeling hot…

You sick? Probably all the wine you drank.

Flushed too…

Seriously… what's happening right now?

I think I'll go strip down and shower. TTYL.

That's dirty, Jenna.

Pretty sure the shower will make me clean.
All those suds…

FML

C ya. XXOO

Jenna tossed her phone on the counter and chewed on her fingernails as she stared at the device. She couldn't believe she'd taken it that far.

Becky's advice was on a loop in her head. Jenna *was* scared of letting someone close because she'd lived in fear for so long. But she was tired of letting her past dictate her future. The innocent flirting through their texting made her feel powerful, not scared.

Jenna grabbed her phone, headed upstairs, and started some laundry before *really* hopping in the shower—that part wasn't a lie. Still tired from her hangover, she slipped on a t-shirt and crawled back into bed.

CHAPTER 13

The week started decent for Jenna, despite the hellacious headache on Sunday. After her flirty texting with Finn, she hadn't heard from him. Jenna tried not to read too much into the radio silence. She knew he was working, so she didn't think it was a ghosting act—she hoped, anyway.

Jenna met Becky in front of her classroom when the last bus pulled off. Bidding farewell to their co-workers, the two women slung their bags over their shoulders and headed toward their cars. The following two days were post-planning, and then they were done for the year.

As Jenna approached her CRV, she noticed something all over the windshield. She gasped when she realized someone had smeared what looked like blood all over her windshield. Then they'd etched the words *You're Mine* into it in some sort of sick prank. Jenna started shaking, unable to control the panic she barely registered as Becky wrapped an arm around her and eased her to the sidewalk. Jenna could vaguely hear Becky talking to someone, but the blood was pumping so loud in her ears that she felt like she was in a tunnel.

"Jenna, stay with me. The police are on their way. Ok? Come on, take some deep breaths. Please…"

Jenna pressed her eyes closed. She wanted to run, hide, anything but sit here on the sidewalk.

Could Alec have found her?

Was he the one doing all these things to her?

She couldn't think, much less take a breath, with the realization Alec could be in Clinton.

FINN HEARD the call regarding vandalism at the school, and something in his gut told him it had to do with Jenna. Flipping on his lights, he rushed to the scene, unsure what he'd find this time.

When he pulled into the parking lot, he was only half prepared for what he saw. Jenna's car was covered in what looked like blood. And as his gaze panned to the sidewalk, he saw Becky trying to console Jenna. Finn barely threw the car in park before his feet hit the ground.

"Becky." He skidded to a stop in front of the two women. "What the hell happened?"

"Oh God, Finn." Becky's face was tear-stained as she stood. "We came out to leave, and we found her car like—" she waved her hand toward the damage. "This. She flipped out— she won't answer me. I think she's having some sort of panic attack."

Finn squatted in front of Jenna and gently placed his hands on her shoulders. "Jenna, it's Finn. Sweetheart, can you hear me?"

Jenna blinked rapidly as her mouth opened and closed like a fish. Tears spilled from the vacant gaze she held, making his heart clench.

Finn brushed his knuckles along her cheek. "Jenna, I'm here. Nothing is going to hurt you. OK? Can you take a deep breath for me?"

His words seemed to do the trick. Her eyes cleared as she took a deep breath. "Finn?"

He cupped her cheek, holding her so her gaze stayed on him. "Yeah, sweetheart. I'm here. Becky called 911. Do you know where you are?"

"I'm…" Jenna pulled from his touch and swiveled her head towards her nearby coworkers. "Oh my god, my car." Her chest heaved with terror, but Finn pulled her hand into his, calming her almost immediately.

"It's ok. We'll get it worked out. Can you stand?" With his help, she pushed to her wobbly legs. "I'm going to take you home, ok?" Finn glanced at Becky. "Can you stay here until the wrecker comes? Officer Davis will be here with you. I want to get her out of here."

"Yeah… sure." Becky turned and leaned into Mr. Harlow, the school principal. Finn noticed the touch was more than professional but didn't call them out. He hated seeing Jenna or his friend shaken up about this.

"Mr. Harlow," Finn glanced toward the man, "Does the school have cameras outside?"

"I'm afraid none that would pick up the staff parking lot. They are only inside the building, at the bus ramp, and right outside the Gym entry on the other side of the building. The badge entry has a camera but only records when a badge is scanned."

"Ok. Thanks. Davis," He looked at his patrolman, "Try not to let the wrecker driver touch the car before investigators arrive. They need to check it for prints."

"Yes, sir. I'll let dispatch know you're tied up as well." The young officer gave him a knowing smile. He knew Finn would not leave Jenna alone.

"Thanks. Come on, Jenna, let me get you home." Finn helped her into his patrol car and buckled her in. She was still in a daze and had uttered nothing beyond a few gasps and muffled sobs. When he slammed the door, Becky rushed over and stopped him.

"Finn, take care of her, please. I've never seen her like this. This whole thing has her terrified."

"Don't worry. I won't let anything happen to her. I promise." His need to protect her had grown tenfold when he saw her on the sidewalk.

Finn knew he would do whatever it took to catch the person responsible for tormenting her.

CHAPTER 14

"Jenna." Finn helped her sit down on the couch. The entire ride over, she'd stayed silent. Finn wasn't sure if she realized he'd brought her to his house—not hers. "Sweetheart," he brushed tendrils of hair out of her face, "Tell me what you need."

She blinked a few times, her gaze scanning the room as she realized she wasn't in her house.

"Finn… This isn't my house."

"I said I was taking you home—I didn't specify whose, though. Let me get you something to drink."

Jenna watched Finn as he crossed into the kitchen. She couldn't help noticing the room was bare, except for a few framed photos on the mantle and a throw blanket on the only other chair. Finn's home was much bigger than she suspected a bachelor like him would need. It was a family home—which made her wonder why a man like him, who didn't want attachments, lived there.

The area she sat in was just off what appeared to be a large, country-style kitchen. Standing, Jenna moved around the room, following the sounds of where Finn had gone.

"Oh… Hey, you didn't have to get up." Finn handed her a glass.

"Finn, I didn't realize you lived in such a big place. It makes mine seem so tiny. What makes a bachelor purchase something this big all for himself?"

"Well…" Finn shifted his gun belt nervously as he walked towards the massive front window. "When I originally bought the place, I thought I'd be starting a family, but—" His eyes held so much pain when he turned toward Jenna briefly, but she watched as he pressed his palm to the glass and stared out into the massive yard. "—sometimes things don't work out."

Jenna could feel the pain in his words. "I'm sorry. It wasn't polite of me to belittle you for living here and being a bachelor. Besides, being single doesn't mean you don't deserve something of your own."

"I didn't think you were belittling me, Jenna, but thank you. You feel up on a tour?"

"You know what? Yes. It will take my mind off other things. Wait…" Jenna pointed at him, "Don't you have to go back to work?"

"No. I called my Captain and took the rest of the night off. He agreed you didn't need to be alone right now."

They held each other's gaze. "Oh." Jenna could feel herself blush under his penetrating gaze.

Despite her earlier breakdown and fucked up situation, Jenna's skin pebbled with awareness of the tension between them.

Finn cleared his throat. "Ah… give me a minute to change, and then I'll show you the place."

Jenna nodded and wandered around while she waited. The kitchen was a cook's dream, adorned with stainless appliances and a large island in the middle. Jenna glanced out the massive sliding glass door and sucked in a breath at the view. His backyard was huge, backing up to a huge pond. Lost in the view's beauty, she nearly shit herself when a large dog jumped against the glass.

He was massive but seemed friendly as he panted and wagged his tail as she eased the door open and let him inside. The dog stood nearly as tall as she did, but he didn't scare Jenna. She had always loved dogs growing up. Jenna dropped to her knees and ran her fingers over his body.

"Well, hello there, handsome."

Jenna plopped down on her butt as the mammoth of fur licked her face. She couldn't stop the giggle from erupting, which only made the dog lick her more.

"Eros, down." Finn stepped into the kitchen, his command causing the dog to sit on Jenna's lap. "Shit, Eros, get off her."

"No… he's fine." Jenna pressed a kiss to the dog's head. "He's gorgeous. Eros?" Jenna raised her brow in question, her lips quirking. "The Greek God of love."

"Yeah—I know it's an odd choice. But when I got him, he was supposed to represent something that turned out to be a lie. By the time I learned what my ex-wife had done—he was already used to his name, and I loved him. Getting rid of him wasn't an option. He's kind of like my kid, you know?"

Eros padded away from Jenna as Finn reached down to help her up. "How about that tour, and then we can talk?"

Jenna nodded and followed Finn through the house. The simple beauty of his place blew her away. Upstairs held four bedrooms, all of which were nicely sized but unfurnished. The last room was the master bedroom. Finn pushed open the door and stepped inside. Jenna gasped at the stark difference between the rest of the house and his room. This room looked like something out of a magazine. The four-poster bed took center stage and was covered in deep burgundy linens. "Wow… it's beautiful."

"Thanks. After my divorce, I burned everything and had to start fresh. Something about this bed called out to me when I saw it, plus it's comfortable."

Jenna ran her hand across the bed. "That's good. Comfort is important."

Finn watched her hands move across his bed, forcing him to stifle a groan. "How about we go downstairs and talk?"

Jenna nodded and walked past him, her body brushing his as she did. Finn's sweats did little to hide the arousal he was feeling just from being close to her and seeing her in his room. With her walking ahead, he attempted to shift himself, tugging his t-shirt down to mask the tent he was sporting. Jenna acted like she hadn't noticed, making Finn grateful, though he'd caught the way her eyes trailed over his body as she walked around him. He followed her into the living room and sat on the coffee table in front of her when she sat down.

"Jenna, I need to know if there is anyone who could mean you harm."

Jenna nodded, looking down at her folded hands. "I thought I'd be safe here. I never thought this would happen. I was sure *he* was a chapter I'd closed when I moved." She took a breath. "I think it was all an illusion… thinking I'd be safe."

"Safe from who, Jenna? You can tell me." Finn reached out and weaved his fingers with her.

"My ex-husband."

CHAPTER 15

OF ALL THE THINGS FINN THOUGHT SHE WOULD SAY, *Ex-husband* was not one of them. He ran his free hand through his hair. "Ex-husband?"

Jenna looked up at him, tears in her eyes as she spoke. "I was married my senior year of college. I'd just turned twenty-one. He was, at least I thought, my prince. But like all fairy tales, it wasn't real, and the prince was, in fact, the villain. The first two years were good, but then he just changed—controlling, accusing, and most of all, abusive. It started small. A bruise here and there, a cut or two, pulling out my hair. You know, the typical stand-up man crap. Then it escalated, as all abuse does. By the time I was twenty-three, I'd suffered broken ribs, broken wrists, a fractured collarbone, and more than a fair share of black eyes." Jenna took a deep breath and continued. "Then, one night, he came home late. He accused me of having an affair with one of my coworkers. There was no reason for the accusation, but it didn't matter. He lost his shit and screamed at me."

Finn watched as the memory washed over her. Jenna's eyes seemed to lose focus as she reached up and brushed her fingers over the back of her head. Her voice was almost a whisper as she continued. "I can still hear the venom in his voice. It haunts my nightmares. He slapped me hard. I can remember thinking, this is it—this is the night he kills me. When he didn't get the reaction he wanted, he hit me again harder. I tried to move away from him… that was my mistake because he punched me. The blow knocked me off my feet, right down the stairs." Jenna let out an uncomfortable laugh.

"It's amazing that I didn't do more than just split my head open… I mean, I was bruised, but nothing broken. Alec had no choice but to take me to the ER, which pissed him off more. They admitted me right away, concerned about head trauma. Alec played the perfect husband, but he did finally leave me in the hospital—work called, and he had no choice but to deal with the problem. Since I'd been admitted, he knew where I'd be when he was done… which meant I couldn't run."

Finn stroked her hand with his thumb, listening as this beautiful woman bared her soul to him. Jenna glanced up, her eyes weary as she finished the story.

"That's when my life was changed forever. An older nurse wouldn't let things go. She stayed with me for hours until I finally admitted to the abuse. She helped me tell my story to the police. Alec was arrested that night—a few months later, he was sentenced to five years, and I was granted a lifetime protection order. Even though he was gone, sitting in a cell, I was afraid of every shadow, every creak. For six months, I went to counseling, and with my therapists' help, I sold the house, moved here, and started over. I thought I'd finally found a new beginning where he couldn't touch me."

Finn brushed a tear from her cheek, his own heart hurting for her. This beautiful woman in front of him had endured the worst possible violence, and yet she kept putting one foot in front of the other. Watching her, Finn stilled when the realization that he wanted to be the man that slayed every one of her dragons washed over him.

Finn whispered, brushing her hair off her face. "What do you mean, you thought you found a new beginning?"

"I got a letter from the Department of Corrections a few days ago. Alec was released early for good behavior. It seems he fooled everyone again."

"Do you think someone in your family told him where you moved?"

She blew out a frustrated sigh. "Not possible. I have no family left. My parents died when I was a freshman in college, and as their only child—well, there's no one who'd have told him. All my information is unlisted. But I have this feeling…" Jenna closed her eyes. She hated to think he'd found her, but the more things happened, the more she couldn't deny he had.

Finn shifted to sit next to her and pulled her into his arms. He held her close to his chest, rubbing her head as he pressed light kissed her forehead lightly. "I won't let anyone hurt you."

Finn held her as she gave into the emotions again. He hated listening to her sobs, but he knew she needed to let it out to let it go. When her cries finally stopped, Finn noticed she'd fallen asleep. Cradling her against his chest, he stood and carried her upstairs to his room. Pulling the covers back, he eased her under them. He covered her body and stood watching her for a few moments. Backing out of his room, he slipped his cell phone from his pocket and called his captain.

"Captain. It's Judson—I need to give you an update about the Hardy case. Seems we might have a lead."

Finn shared her entire story, leaving no detail out. He was sick to his stomach recounting the things she'd told him. By the time he was done, fury had consumed both men. His captain confirmed that Alec had been released; worse, he never checked in with his parole officer.

Jenna's worst fear was likely coming true. Everything pointed to her ex being responsible for the vandalism and threats.

Glancing at the time on his phone, he was shocked to see it was almost seven. He and Jenna spent nearly three hours talking. It was no wonder she'd worn herself out.

Finn figured she'd be hungry, so he headed into the kitchen to throw something together. He'd wake her and then tell her what he'd found out.

CHAPTER 16

Jenna came awake slowly, slightly disoriented by her surroundings. Stretching, she shook the sleep from her eyes and smiled. She was in Finn's bed. Sliding her feet to the floor, she padded to his bathroom and splashed water onto her face. Her reflection looked as bad as she felt. Deciding there was nothing she could change about her current state, she left the safety of Finn's bathroom. Easing the bedroom door open, she was assaulted by the most delicious scent.

The smell made her mouth water, and her stomach growl in response. Hurrying down the stairs, she stopped at the sight of Finn standing at the stove. He had soft music playing as he stood before a pan stirring. Something splattered from the contents, causing Finn to jump back. He let out a string of swear words as he stripped his shirt off. Jenna inhaled a sharp breath at the sight of him shirtless. His back was muscular, topped with strong, broad shoulders, one of which displayed the start of a tattoo that weaved down his arm.

Finn must have heard her because he looked over his shoulder and smiled at her. "I didn't hear you come in. Hungry?"

"Um… yeah."

"Come. Sit." He pointed to one of the stools at the island in the middle of the kitchen. Finn set a plate down in front of Jenna. "Hope you like stir-fry."

"I'm so hungry it wouldn't matter, but yes, I do." Jenna took a bite, moaning as the flavors assaulted her senses. "*Fuck. This is good.*"

Finn couldn't take his eyes off her as she ate. Every groan, every hiss she made sent a jolt straight to his cock. The timing was terrible, but he couldn't help his reactions—she made eating sexy. Finn barely touched his food because he was too caught up watching her.

He hadn't realized it until Jenna said something. "You not gonna to eat?" She spoke over a mouthful of food, using her fork to point at his half-eaten plate of food.

"Yeah… got distracted for a minute." Finn shoveled his food in as fast as he could chew. "So," he mumbled as he swallowed the last bite. "We need to talk about a couple of things."

"That sounds ominous." Jenna pushed her plate away from her. "But nothing can be worse after having my car covered in what I hope was paint." She watched as Finn shifted nervously on his stool. "Oh. God. It's worse, isn't it?"

Finn reached across the table and grabbed her hand. "I'm not sure, but it could be. I called my Captain and told him about your past. He did some digging and discovered that your ex-husband didn't check in with his parole officer after his release."

Jenna's grip on his hand tightened, and a myriad of emotions fluttered across her face as he continued. "We don't know if that means he's found you, and there is zero evidence that shows the recent vandalism was his doing." Finn ran his thumb across her knuckles. "But we need to consider it could be him. And that means we need to think about your safety until whoever is doing this slips up. Ok?"

"What does that even mean, Finn? I can't afford a security system or a bodyguard. Can't the police department just put a watch on my house?"

"Yes, but that's not enough. You shouldn't stay at your house for a while."

"Jesus Christ!"

Jenna jerked her hand from his and stood, knocking the chair to the floor. She stormed into the living room, causing Eros to perk up from his slumber on the couch. Jenna plopped down beside him and began stroking his head.

"Look, I know you're pissed. I'm livid about what you endured—you didn't deserve to be treated that way. No woman does, Jenna. But we need to ensure he isn't doing this, which means giving up your freedom for a little while. We need to make sure you're safe—*I* need to make sure you're safe. Ok?" Finn sat down next to her and tugged her free hand into his. "I want you to stay here in my house."

"Finn—" Finn pressed his finger to her lips, silencing her. Jenna tried to pull her hand free, but he tightened his hold. "Hear me out. You can stay in one of the guest rooms—I'll buy a bed today. I'll give you a key, so you don't have to rely on me to get in and out. But I will ask you to let me know where you're going. Please, Jenna. I can protect you here. Plus, Eros seems to have fallen in love with you." The pup lifted his head and licked Jenna's hand as if on cue. "He can keep watch as well."

"I can't do that, Finn. I appreciate your concern, but do you think my place is unsafe?"

"Someone has damaged your car, not once but twice, while it was parked in your driveway—not to mention the threatening message left for you at your place of work. Yes, I believe your place is unsafe. And sure, the department can have someone do zone patrols, but they're inconsistent and won't stop someone from hurting you. *Please*, Jenna."

Jenna looked down at Eros because she could not look at Finn and ask the question burning in her chest. "Why are you doing this, Finn? I'm nobody to you... you don't owe me anything."

"I won't pretend you coming here isn't, on some level, for selfish reasons. But with everything that's happened, I have this innate desire to see to your safety. Being here will satisfy that need without losing my mind."

Jenna lifted her head, her gaze meeting his. "What do you mean... selfish reasons?"

"You know damn well what it means. I respect that you said you weren't in a place for a relationship—I see why now. But that doesn't mean I won't stop chasing you, Jenna. We have some serious chemistry between us if the kisses we've shared are any indicator. I'm a patient man. I can wait until you're at a place to accept what I'm willing to give. However, in the meantime… I need you here, *please*."

Jenna stroked Eros, his head resting comfortably in her lap. She couldn't deny that she felt utterly safe around Finn. She also couldn't help but think staying here would lead to her letting down her barriers and giving in to her desire for him. But as she sat there thinking about everything—her fear won. She didn't want to go home to jump at every shadow.

Sighing, "Fine. I'll stay for a few days to see if your department can determine who is doing this. I'll need to go home and grab a couple of things. I still have two days of work left. Shit." Jenna froze. "How the hell am I supposed to get to work?"

"You can use my car. I have a take-home car for work, so my Charger sits most of the time."

"No, I can't take your car. I wouldn't feel comfortable driving it. Can't you give me a ride to the school? Becky can bring me home after."

"Fine… If it makes you feel better, I can do that. I don't go in until nine, anyway. Alright," Finn stood, holding his hands out to her. "Let's go get your things. It's getting late." Finn tugged Jenna to her feet.

"Finn," Jenna whispered, realizing he was still shirtless. "You should probably put on a shirt."

CHAPTER 17

Jenna couldn't stop fidgeting during the ride to her house. As they pulled into her driveway, she immediately noticed her door was cracked.

"What the hell?" Finn put his hand on her leg. "Stay in the car and call 911."

He reached across her and pulled a gun from his glove box. Jenna could see him switching to cop mode as he slipped from the car. "Lock the door until I come back."

"Can't you wait until another officer gets here? What if someone is inside, Finn? You could get hurt." She couldn't stop the panic welling in her gut.

"I'll be fine. Just stay here."

He pushed the car door shut and shuffled towards the front door of Jenna's house. Finn's head was on swivel, and he had his gun ready. It was apparent where her deadbolt had been pried open with something. Scrapes and damage to the wood told him this wasn't someone with a key. Not to mention, the ring doorbell was smashed to pieces on the porch at his feet. Carefully edging the door open with his shoe, he eased inside. The house was cast in shadows, the sun nearly buried beneath the horizon.

Finn called out, "Police… anyone here?"

He waited. His breath held tight in his chest as he listened for any sounds. Letting out the air burning his lungs, Finn eased around the open living room into the kitchen.

Once he was sure no one was on the first floor, he took the stairs, careful not to make any sound. He was grateful her stairs didn't creak under his weight, giving his presence away. Checking the first two rooms, Finn found them empty.

He paused outside Jenna's bedroom and listened. Hearing nothing, he pushed the door open, his gun drawn. His stomach lurched in his throat at what he found. Her room had been completely trashed. Finn quickly went to the attached bathroom, clearing it of any hidden danger. Stepping back into her bedroom, Finn found the light switch and flicked it on, basking her room in the light.

Whoever had broken in has destroyed the tiny space. Her bed had been shredded, cotton spilling from the linens and mattress—more disturbing was the same red paint used to vandalize her car was spilled across the room. On the only bare wall, someone had written her a message that made his stomach roll unease.

"Finn?" He jumped when he heard her call his name from downstairs.

"Stay there!" He called out as he darted into the hall. "Jenna, I told you to wait outside." Finn caught sight of the patrol officer behind her. "Officer Davis."

He was relieved to see it was the same officer who'd responded to the school earlier.

Jenna started up the stairs, Davis on her tail. "Did you find anything?" Jenna tried to step into her room, but Finn stopped her.

"Sweetheart." He pulled her to his chest, "You don't need to see this. Davis, get a detective out here."

"What? Finn, you're scaring me." She pulled from him, shoving past his muscular frame, and stumbled into her room.

Jenna's eyes scanned the mess, stopping at the disgusting message painted into the sheetrock.

Keep running… eventually, you'll be mine.

"Oh my God."

Finn watched as crocodile tears spilled down her cheeks, and her body shook with emotion.

"Come here." Finn thumbed the wetness on her cheek and tucked her against his side. "Let's go downstairs and wait on the detective. You shouldn't be in here—we've already contaminated the crime scene enough."

Jenna nodded, letting Finn guide her from the room and down the stairs. He led her to the couch and sat down with her.

"Why is this happening?" Jenna leaned her head into her hands. Finn pressed his hand to her back, his heart breaking with every sob that echoed through the room.

"Hey… we'll figure this out."

"Sergeant Judson." Detective Peterson stepped into the living room. "Can we talk outside for a minute?"

Finn glanced over his shoulder at the brooding man, "Yeah. Jenna, stay here. I'll be right back."

Finn slipped out front with the detective. "Peterson, did you see the room?" Finn asked as he pushed the door closed.

"Yeah—it's fucked up. Captain filled me in, and I've done some digging. I'm pretty sure this is her ex-husband." Peterson ran his hand through his salt and pepper hair. "But with no physical evidence tying him to these crimes, it will be hard to prove. Plus, no one has seen him. Finn, I don't need to tell you this rarely ends well. She's not safe here."

"She's staying with me."

Peterson's gaze bored into him. "I see. You sure that's smart?"

Finn growled, his fist balling at his sides. "What the fuck does that mean?"

"Finn... don't let your feelings for her get in the way. She's been hurt—bad. I had her file sent over from her hometown and what I saw there." Peterson sighed. "Let's just say it's amazing she's not dead already."

Finn squeezed his eyes shut. Jenna had already told him about the abuse, but hearing his co-worker confirm the severity made his body vibrate with rage. "She's got no one, Peterson. What's she supposed to do?"

"You're wrong about that... Pretty sure she has you. Just don't let feelings for her beyond your job get in the way, ok?"

"Yeah. Fine. I need to get back to her. We need to get some of her things. Is it ok if we go in the room?"

"I don't know if she needs to see it again. I'm not sure she saw what was written, but yeah, just as soon as we're done taking pictures."

Finn nodded and slipped back inside. Jenna was still sitting on the couch, staring at the wall. Finn hated seeing her so fragile. Peterson was right. He had feelings for her, but her safety was more important than how he felt, so he would need to push those aside for now.

"Hey." Finn crouched in front of her. "I can go grab your clothes. Just tell me what you need."

"I can come."

"Jenna, I don't think you need to see your room again. Seriously, I can do it."

Jenna stood, "I'll be alright."

Finn hesitated, but he could tell she wouldn't listen. Together, they climbed the stairs, and he watched as she stepped inside. He pressed his hand to her back when she tensed, gently guiding her to the closet. She snapped out of her semi-trance and started grabbing clothes. After filling a suitcase with things from her closet and dresser, she cleared out her bathroom.

Finn's heart broke as he took her luggage and tossed them into his trunk. Jenna sunk into the passenger seat and slumped her body against the window. Glancing at the house one last time, he backed out and drove them home.

CHAPTER 18

Jenna didn't remember the drive or walking into the house. One minute, she was staring at the vile things written on her bedroom wall; the next, she was looking at Finn's massive bed.

"Jenna." Finn's hand rested on her back. "I put your luggage in my closet and your toiletries on the bathroom counter. Why don't you lie down—try to get some sleep."

Jenna glanced around, realizing what he was saying. "What? No, I can't take your room, Finn."

"Yes, you can. I'll sleep downstairs on the couch. Unfortunately, I didn't furnish the other rooms, so this is the only bed for now. You'll sleep better in it, ok?"

Jenna nodded, unable to answer. Finn was like something from a fairy tale, something she didn't deserve.

"I'm going to let Eros out and grab you some water. Change, get comfortable, whatever… I'll be right back." Finn pressed a chaste kiss to her forehead and ducked out of the room.

Jenna closed her eyes. Her life was a nightmare. A nightmare she thought she'd left behind. Blinking, she stepped to the bed and kicked off her shoes. She didn't feel like hunting through her clothes, so she shucked her shorts, removed her bra, and slipped under the covers.

His mattress was like sleeping on a cloud—a cloud that smelled like aftershave and dryer sheets. Burrowing her head into his pillow, she inhaled the scent. The way his scent calmed her made her crave it. It traveled through her nervous system, causing the tension in her body to relax. Finn appeared beside the bed, carrying a bottle of water.

"Here, in case you get thirsty." He set the cold plastic bottle on the side table. "I'm going to take a quick shower, then let you get some rest."

Jenna watched as he tucked himself behind the bathroom door. She listened as the sound of the water kicked on. Her mind immediately conjured a visual of a very naked Finn soaking wet. Shaking her head, she grabbed and guzzled the water, trying to quell the heat coursing through her. Setting the bottle back down, she turned off the light and sunk deeper into the covers. Closing her eyes, she willed herself to stop thinking about Finn naked a few feet away.

FINN PUSHED the door shut and turned on the shower. Leaning against the counter, he stared at his reflection in the mirror. Thinking about Jenna in his bed sent the blood straight to his cock. Huffing out a breath, he pleaded with his conscience to get control. She didn't need him lusting after her—she needed him to protect her. Stepping into the stall, he let the hot water wash over his body. His hands braced against the cool tile as he squeezed his eyes shut. His dick had other ideas and was at attention. He knew he couldn't step out with his dick on high alert—hell, he didn't want to embarrass himself. He turned the water to cold, the temperature change having the effect he'd hoped for. Quickly washing off, he stepped out and grabbed a towel.

"Shit."

He'd forgotten to grab clothes before heading into the bathroom. He was so used to living alone that it hadn't crossed his mind. Toweling off, he wrapped the white cotton snug around his waist. Easing the door open, he peeked out, pleased to find Jenna appeared to be asleep. Slipping into the cool room, he quickly grabbed a pair of boxer briefs and slipped them on under his towel.

"*NO.*" The high-pitched sound, a cross between a moan and a cry, caused Finn to drop his towel and turn.

He found Jenna tossing and turning in what appeared to be a nightmare. Finn rushed to the bedside and sat down.

"Jenna." He gently laid his hand on her shoulder.

"PLEASE… No… Don't…"

His gut clenched with each cry from her lips. "Jenna, sweetheart, wake up." He ran his hand down her cheek.

Jenna sucked in a breath as she was startled awake. She stared at him with unfocused eyes, still half-asleep.

"Finn?" She was disoriented as she looked around the room, confused.

"You were having a nightmare."

"A nightmare…" she shook her head, her eyes closing. "Fuck."

"Hey… it's ok. You're safe. Let me get you something to help you sleep." Finn shifted, Jenna, snagging his wrist as he stood.

"Can you… do you think?" She blushed, "Can you just lay with me?"

Finn tried to hide his shock. "If that's what you want."

"Please, I feel safer when you're here. I think it'll help me sleep."

"If you're sure." Finn pulled his hand free and stepped around to the other side. He pulled the covers back and slipped in beside her. Jenna rolled to her side, pressing her back to him.

"Thank you, Finn."

Finn stayed on his back, praying his body would behave. "No problem. Try to sleep, Jenna. I'll be right here."

Finn stared at the ceiling. The light from the bathroom was still on as it spilled into the bedroom, casting a yellow glow into the room's darkness. Jenna's soft breaths told him she was finally asleep again. Jenna shifted, rolling her body against his. Finn sucked in a breath when she wedged her leg between his, pressing her chest into his side.

Finn tensed. "Jenna," he whispered her name into the dark as his hand pressed into her shoulder.

"Humm?" She grumbled in her sleepy state. Her eyes cracked open, and her body stiffened when she realized what she'd done. "Oh my god… Finn, I'm so sorry."

She shifted, her leg rubbing against his manhood. There was no way to hide his reaction to her. With her body pressed against him, she'd woken his damn cock up.

"Sorry…" Finn tried to shift away, but Jenna clenched her leg, locking him still.

"Finn." Jenna pressed into him harder, grinding her warm center against his bare leg.

"Jenna," Finn growled. "What are you doing?"

"I—" Her hand slid down his abs, stopping at the top of his briefs.

Finn grabbed her hand. "We shouldn't do this, Jenna. You're just confused."

"I'm not confused. Please make me forget the bad stuff, Finn. I thought you were attracted to me."

"More than you know, Jenna. Which is why I can be something you use to forget." He tried to shift away, but her hold tightened more.

"I don't want to use you to forget, Finn. I want you to show me how it's supposed to be." She whispered the words, driving a hammer through the walls he'd erected to protect her.

"Damn it, Jenna." Finn flipped them over, pinning her beneath his body. "I *am* attracted to you." He pressed his engorged cock against her, causing her to moan. "But you've been through a shitload of trauma, and I don't want to take advantage of you."

Jenna shifted, thrusting her hips up against the stiff ridge of his cock. "Finn. I'm thinking clearly. This isn't you taking advantage of me… this is you finally *getting* me."

CHAPTER 19

Jenna slipped her hand between them, shoving the material covering his rock-hard shaft, and freed his dick. Finn sucked in a sharp breath as Jenna rubbed the pre-cum around the head of his cock with her thumb. Finn shifted away, settling between her legs as his shaft pressed at the apex of her legs.

"Please." She wrapped her legs around him, causing the head of his cock to brush against her core.

"Fuck." He inhaled a hiss. "Are you sure?"

"Yes."

That was all Finn needed. He shoved his hand between them, ripping her panties off, and tossed them to the floor. He slid his palm beneath her ass and buried his shaft inside her.

"Fuck, you're so wet, baby." He paused, giving her time to adjust and himself a minute to gain control.

Jenna tossed her head back and moaned, her heels digging into his ass, shoving him deeper. Finn eased his shaft out, then slammed back into her.

"YES... *please*."

Her screams sent him into a frenzy. Their bodies molded together as he thrust into her. The sound of flesh slapping against flesh filled his bedroom. Finn slipped his hand beneath her shirt, finding her bare breast. He squeezed, pinching the taunt nipple before pushing the cotton up so he could take the sweet bud in his mouth. Jenna let out a scream, her pussy contracting as her orgasm washed over her.

"That's it, baby. Give it to me. Let me feel you come all over my cock." He pressed his lips to hers, kissing her with a fierceness he'd never felt before. Jenna clawed at his back, panting as he continued his assault on her womb.

"I'm going to come again..." She moaned, her legs locking onto his body. He felt his release building as his balls slapped against her ass.

"FUCK!" Finn grunted as he pumped into her. Jenna let out another scream, her pussy swallowing his shaft as his come spurted inside her channel. Finn's body convulsed as he continued spilling inside her.

Finally, Finn collapsed, rolling onto his back and pulling Jenna into his arms. Their ragged breaths filled the room as they tried to calm their racing hearts.

"I didn't mean for that to happen, Jenna." Finn's deep voice cut through the shadowed room. "But... I won't lie—I've wanted you for a while now, so I don't regret a minute. Are you ok?"

Jenna nestled into his side. "I fought this attraction, afraid to let myself trust the feelings. But you make me feel safe, Finn. And I wanted this to happen just as much as you did. Please don't apologize." Jenna pressed a kiss to his warm skin. "I needed to feel in control of something."

Finn let out a chuckle. "Well, you can control me anytime you want, Jenna. And you don't need to be afraid. I'll protect you—and your heart."

Jenna swirled her fingertips across Finn's taunt muscles. "Your ex-wife was a dumbass."

Finn stiffened beneath her, his hand tightening on her side. "What?"

"You're a good man, Finn. She was stupid to walk away from your marriage. But I need to thank her—because I wouldn't be here right now if she hadn't. I don't know why you're with me... lord knows I have some serious baggage."

"You don't give yourself any credit, Jenna. What happened with your ex wasn't your fault. And I should thank him as well—because you're mine now."

Finn could feel Jenna smile against him. "Thank you."

He squeezed her tighter, pressing a kiss to her head. "Get some sleep... I'll be right here holding you."

Jenna closed her eyes. The warmth of his body against hers gave her a sense of comfort she hadn't felt in a long time. She'd never felt this close to anyone, not even when she was married before it all went to hell. A part of her was afraid, but not in the way she'd been with Alec. No, this time, she was scared of how much she needed Finn and wanted him.

When his breaths finally slowed and became steady, Jenna let herself drift off to sleep. Her dreams were filled with something she'd never experienced before… love.

CHAPTER 20

Jenna woke wrapped in a blanket of arms and legs. She smiled, realizing the night before hadn't been a dream. Flashes of her and Finn tangled together caused her cheeks to blush. She carefully slipped out from under his arm and stood. She couldn't help but stare at his naked form on the bed. Finn was like a dream to her. His body was sculpted to perfection. Smiling, she tip-toed to the bathroom to shower. It was nearly six in the morning, and despite the events from the day before, she had two days left of work.

Jenna turned on the water and stepped in once it turned hot. The heat of the spray washed over her as she dipped her head beneath the shower head. Her mind was lost in thought when she was startled by solid arms wrapping around her.

Jenna nearly jumped out of her skin as she spun away from him. "Shit—Jenna, I'm sorry. I didn't mean to scare you." Finn pulled her against his naked chest. He could feel her heart pounding against his.

"It's alright—I guess I'm still jumpy." Jenna wiggled against him, smiling when she felt his manhood pressing against her belly. Their height difference was considerable, making the top of his erection rest between the bottom of her breasts. Jenna glanced up at Finn. "Good morning."

"Sorry—he has a mind of his own sometimes. What are you doing awake?"

"I have work."

"Jenna—I am sure your principal doesn't expect you to come in, considering the situation. Plus, it probably isn't safe."

"Oh no. I will not let this force me into hiding. The school is secure. I won't be going anywhere but my classroom to close for the summer."

"I don't like it—it makes you vulnerable."

"You can take me and pick me up."

"Jenna…" Finn's words were halted when Jenna wrapped her lips around the crown of his dick. "Fuck." He pressed his hand against the shower wall, his head tilting toward the ceiling as she swallowed him down.

Jenna fisted his cock, jerking him off as she licked and sucked. Her free hand gripped his ass, pulling him closer as she bobbed her head.

Finn's body tensed as her lips glided over his sensitive head. She licked her way down his shaft, sucking his balls into her mouth. Finn bucked his hips.

"Woman…" he reached down, tugging her arms to pull her up. Lifting her body, Jenna wrapped her legs around his waist as Finn pressed his lips to hers. Their kiss was heated and frantic. Finn's cock was poised at her entrance as he backed her against the tile. He sucked her bottom lip into his mouth, nibbling the tender flesh. Jenna arched into his chest as he licked his way to the hollow of her neck.

"Please…" Her plea made his cock grow harder. "Fuck me, Finn." Jenna wiggled until his cock was dipping into her folds. Her body was wet with need. Finn bucked his hips, burying himself inside her warm walls.

He thrust in and out, their bodies pressed against the tile. The water cascaded over them, the steam filling the tiny stall as Finn held onto Jenna. Jenna moaned, her body responding to his as if they were one. "Oh God, that's it, Finn. Please, right there…yes…yes…oh…" He could feel her womb clenching as she neared her peak.

"Fuck, Jenna. You feel so good wrapped around my cock." Jenna bounced, meeting each thrust with vigor. "You like it when I talk dirty? That's it, baby, fuck my dick. Milk it dry.' Finn grunted his release building. "Give it to me, Jenna. Let me feel you take it all."

"OH… FINN!" Jenna screamed his name, her pussy clamping down on his swollen member. Her pussy pulsed and spasmed. And despite the water from the shower, Finn could feel the warmth of her orgasm covering his cock.

"That's it… that's what I want." Finn slipped his hand beneath their wet bodies and thumbed her clit. Pinching and twisting it, "I want one more, Jenna."

"I can't, Finn… oh god…"

"You can, baby. I want you to come with me once more. Fuck my dick, Jenna. You know you want it." Finn moved their bodies, stepping toward the massive bench in the stall. He sat down, shifting Jenna to straddle him, and pressed himself deeper into her womb.

Jenna leaned her head back, moaning as he thrust his cock inside her. She moved against him, her clit rubbing against his pubic bone. Finn grabbed her head, pulling her lips to his. His hand slid between them, his thumb pressing against the sensitive nub. Jenna moaned into his lips, her movements becoming more frantic.

"I'm going to come… Oh, GOD… FUCK… Fuck… Finn… Oh… Please…" Her cries made him mad with lust. Finn pumped his hips, driving himself deeper. Gripping her hips, he moved her body with his.

"Fuck… come with me, Jenna… That's it, baby…" Jenna clenched her legs, tightening her cunt around his cock. "FUCK…" Finn closed his eyes, his orgasm bursting from him like a volcanic eruption. His hips twitched, jerking into Jenna as his come spilled out. Jenna let out a scream, her orgasm ripping from her as they came together. Finn rested his forehead against hers. "Damn, woman. You're going to kill me."

Jenna laughed as he held her. "Good morning to you, too." She eased herself off his lap. "Guess I need to finish getting clean."

Finn stood with her, helping her steady on her feet. He grabbed the shampoo and began scrubbing his hands through her hair. Neither spoke as they took turns washing each other. Finn cut the shower off when the water ran cold and wrapped Jenna in a towel. He quickly dried himself off and scooped her up in his arms.

"I'll take you to work. I don't like it, but I won't stop you."

"Thank you, Finn." She kissed his lips. "Now, can you put me down? I need to get dressed."

"Not yet." He carried her into the bedroom and laid her down on the bed. "I need to be inside you one more time."

Finn took her slowly, savoring every inch of her body. Jenna hurried to get dressed when they finished, knowing she would be late, but she didn't care.

Being with Finn made her feel something she was scared to admit. As they backed out of the driveway, Jenna glanced at Finn, loving how happy he looked.

Catching her staring at him, he shot her a sexy grin. "I need to run by the station, but I'll be back in a few hours. Don't leave the school—ok?"

"I won't, I promise." Finn squeezed her hand, pulling it to his lips as he kissed her knuckles. Jenna smiled, her gut tightening with what felt a lot like love.

Jenna swore she'd never give a man her heart again, but looking at Finn as he drove, she knew she was doomed. Turning her head, she glanced out the window and accepted that she was falling in love with him. And that scared her more than being stalked by her psycho ex-husband.

CHAPTER 21

After Finn dropped Jenna off and spoke to David Harlow, the school's principal, he headed towards the station. Something had changed in the car on the way to the school. He'd felt the shift in Jenna's mood but didn't ask her about it. He thought she was trying to hide her fear, but he couldn't be sure. She said little, and when he kissed her goodbye, there was trepidation in her eyes.

Finn headed straight for the Captain's office. "Captain?" Finn pushed into the tiny space. "You got a second?"

"Finn. I was just about to call and check in with you. How's Miss Hardy?"

"Good. I just dropped her off at the school."

"What? She went in to work?"

"I know… I tried to convince her to stay home, but she's stubborn. Years of being controlled by her ex has made her even more determined to be strong."

"Probably true. Well, unfortunately, whoever vandalized her house didn't leave any prints. They must have been wearing gloves. I put a man on her house, though, to see if anyone came back by. The weird thing is the video doorbell had been smashed. Whoever did this to her place knew it was there or had enough sense to get rid of the damn thing."

"It's got to be the ex." Finn sat down in the seat across from Hutchens.

"Yeah—that's what Peterson thinks. We still have found nothing on his whereabouts. His parole officer is helping us with that as well. She still staying at your place?"

"Yes," Finn answered, hastier than he'd intended.

"I see." Hutchens raised an eyebrow. "Is there something going on between you two?"

Finn glanced up at his friend and boss. "I'm not sure. I mean," he ran his palm down his face, "I care about this girl —more than I should. I have for a while now—even before this mess, but she wouldn't give me the time of day. Of course, now I know why. But…"

"But now she's leaning on you, and you're unsure if it's because she wants to or has to. Am I right?"

"Yeah—I guess so. I don't know what will happen when this is over, which scares me."

"Wow…" Hutchens folded his hands on the desk. "You're in love with this woman."

"What? No. I mean, I care about her…" Finn stopped. *Love?* Finn thought about her in his arms. He thought about how he felt when she was scared and let him hold her. Then he thought about how he felt sitting there, away from her. His heart sped up, beating hard against his chest. *"Fuck."*

"Yep, you're screwed."

Finn glanced at his friend. "What do I do?"

"Tell her, Finn. And keep her with you. Knowing how you feel, you're the best person to protect her. I don't know how long this will last, but she is a walking target for some weirdo — her ex or not."

"Alright. Well, I should get back to her. I don't want to leave her alone too long."

"Keep me posted."

Finn nodded, walking out to his car. His chest constricted when he thought about Captain's words.

He was in love with Jenna Hardy.

Now, he just needed to figure out when to tell her. The last thing he wanted was to scare her off. He didn't need her to leave just yet—not until she was safe and this was over. Finn decided he'd keep his feelings to himself until the threat had passed. Then, he would lay it all out for her.

And maybe, just maybe, she'd give him a real chance.

CHAPTER 22

"Jenna," Mr. Harlow greeted her. "Look, considering everything, you didn't need to come to work."

"I know, Mr. Harlow, but I needed to. I can't let fear control me anymore. I promised Finn I would stay inside. I want to get my room closed for the summer."

"Fine—but if you need something or well…" he paused. "Let me know how I can help, ok?" He tugged her into a hug.

Jenna tensed; the show of affection made her uncomfortable. "Sure. Thanks. I'll let you know when I am done." She pulled from his awkward embrace and smiled.

"Becky should be in her room. Go see her. She's been worried about you."

"I will." Jenna noticed how his face glowed when he spoke her name. Jenna suspected something more between them, but Becky had said nothing to her about it. She hurried down the hall, seeking her friend's room.

"Becky," Jenna walked into the empty classroom.

"JENNA!" Becky rushed to her, throwing her arms around Jenna, and squeezed.

"Jeez, woman, you're crushing me." Jenna laughed.

"Oh, my god! I've been so worried about you..." Becky broke the embrace and searched her friend over. "You look good. Are you ok?"

"Ironically, I am."

"Wait, why are you here? I thought for sure you'd take off today."

"Finn wanted me to, but I needed to come in. I couldn't let someone control me like that."

"Finn, huh? He sure went all alpha male on everyone yesterday. I don't think I've ever seen him get so protective of anyone—not even his ex-wife." Becky smiled. She'd known Finn long enough to notice something like that.

Jenna blushed. "He's been...helpful."

"Probably because you got some of that golden dick."

Jenna's face grew redder. "Umm..."

"HOLY SHIT... I was kidding. He fucking took advantage of you while you were vulnerable... I can't believe this..."

"Actually..." Jenna smiled, "I took advantage of him. I needed to erase the awful nightmare I'd had—so I asked him to lie down with me last night. And... well, I couldn't help myself."

"JENNA... you naughty girl..."

"Yeah—he refused at first. Saying I wasn't in the right place for something physical. But I didn't take no for an answer, and his dick agreed with me. So…"

"You slut… well, was it good?" Becky slapped Jenna's shoulder, and her laughter made Jenna smile wider.

"It was the best sex I've ever had, Becky. He was unbelievable. And then this morning," Jenna closed her eyes; the memory of their bodies tangled in the shower and then in the bed filled her head.

"Whoa, wait a minute. You slept with him more than once?"

Jenna beamed, her face flush with desire as she thought about Finn's body pressed against hers. "Becky, it scares me how he makes me feel."

"What do you mean?"

"I swore I'd never let another man in after Alec. But there is something about Finn that makes me believe—" Jenna paused.

"Makes you believe what? You know, not all men are like Alec. Finn is a great guy. And it's obvious he cares about you. He's been trying to get you to go out with him since you moved here."

"I know… but he deserves someone better than me. I have so much baggage. After what his ex-wife did to him, he deserves a woman that doesn't carry so much darkness."

"Jenna," Becky placed her hand on Jenna's arm, "You deserve some happiness, and Finn can give you that. What are you afraid of?"

"Not being loved back."

CHAPTER 23

FINN STOOD OUTSIDE BECKY'S CLASSROOM DOOR. HE DIDN'T mean to eavesdrop but hadn't wanted to interrupt Jenna. He couldn't believe she felt so worthless. His years of experience on the force told him domestic violence took a toll on a woman's self-esteem, but to hear it from her lips was a gut punch. What he didn't expect was her fear of not being loved back. Did that mean she felt that way for him? Finn smiled at the thought that maybe she felt more for him than just being her protector.

He cleared his throat as she stepped into the room. "Becky, Jenna." He smiled at his longtime friend.

"Finn!" Becky hugged him. "How long have you been here?" She smiled, knowing he'd heard their conversation. Jenna's eyes widened, embarrassment riddling her body.

"Just got here. Didn't want to leave Jenna alone too long."

"Awe, that's sweet of you. We were talking about you."

"Becky." Jenna's voice filled with warning as she cut her eyes towards her friend.

"Sweetheart," Finn turned toward her. "Need any help to get your room packed?"

"Um…" she shook her head as the memory of him under the shower spray assaulted her vision. "Sure… yes. Thank you. Becky, I'll see you later."

Jenna walked past Finn, heading toward her room down the hall. Finn followed her into the dark classroom, pushing the door closed as he grabbed her wrist. He spun her around, pressing her back against the cool wood. His lips found hers as he wedged his knee between her legs. Jenna moaned into his mouth, their tongues tangling in a sensual kiss.

Finn released her, reaching behind her and flicking the switch to fill the room with light. "Now, let's get started." He released her body, leaving her wanting more.

Jenna sighed, her center tingling with need. Finn did things to her body that she couldn't explain. "Ok."

Jenna and Finn worked the next couple of hours packing up her room. Jenna sat down on a desk. "Well, that went faster than I expected. It's not even two yet." She smiled.

"I'm starving. Let's grab a late lunch and head home." Finn took her hand in his and tugged her to stand.

"I just need to let Mr. Harlow know I'm leaving."

"Ok, we'll stop by his office on the way out."

Jenna stepped into the hall. "Let me say goodbye to Becky first."

Jenna abruptly stopped in Becky's doorway, causing Finn to ram into her. "Shit." he grabbed her hips, steadying her. "Why'd you sto—" Finn smiled when he saw the cause for Jenna's quick halt.

Becky was wrapped in a steamy embrace with Mr. Harlow. He had her backed against her desk, poised between her legs. Becky's hands were threaded through his hair, neither of them aware of Finn nor Jenna's presence.

Finn coughed, signaling the two to their arrival. Becky jerked back, "Oh, shit."

"Um, I just wanted to let you know I was leaving. I finished my room."

Mr. Harlow froze, never turning around. "Good… don't worry about coming in tomorrow. You take care of yourself."

Becky peered around his tall frame and mouthed. "Call me later."

"Ok… see you, guys." Jenna blushed, Finn tugging her out of the door. "Holy shit."

"Yeah—didn't see that coming. Let's go. I'm hungry." Jenna nodded, threading her fingers through his as they walked down the hall and out of the building.

Finn helped her into the car, kissing her head before shutting the door. Jenna and Finn headed towards his house after a quick stop at the local diner. When they pulled into the drive-way, Jenna saw Finn tense.

"What is it?"

"Eros…" Finn pointed towards the front door. Eros lay on the front porch, unmoving.

"Oh my God." Jenna bolted from the car before Finn had even come to a complete stop.

"Jenna!" Finn threw it in park. "Wait!"

Jenna ignored him, racing up the steps and dropping to her knees next to the beast of a dog. Her hands went to his side, feeling for a sign of life. Eros let out a slight whine, signaling he wasn't dead.

"Eros," Jenna pulled her hands back to find them coated in red as Finn kneeled beside her. "He's bleeding…"

"Jenna, help me get him in the car." Finn slid his hands beneath the dog's body, scooping him to his chest. "Get the door."

Jenna ran ahead of him, opening the passenger door and sliding into the seat. "Here, lay him on my lap." Finn stood beside the door.

"He'll crush you."

"I don't care. Give him to me." Finn slipped him to her, slamming the door closed, and rushed to the driver's side.

"It's ok, buddy. Hang on."

"Who did this to him?"

"I don't know." Finn ran his hands over his furry friend's head. "I need to make a call." He slipped his cell phone out and pressed the speaker.

"Hutchens." The gruff voice of Captain Hutchens filled the car.

"Captain. I need a unit to my house."

"Finn? What happened?"

"I don't know. I'm headed to the vet—someone stabbed my dog and left him for dead on the front porch."

"What the fuck!"

"Look, we weren't there. I do not know if someone's still there or not. We snatched up Eros and left."

"You take care of your dog, Finn. I'll go over to your house myself. Keep me updated."

"Will do."

Finn disconnected the call, his hand resting on Eros. Jenna covered his hand with hers. "He'll be ok."

Finn smiled at Jenna as he tried to hide his tears. Eros was like his child, and losing him would tear him apart.

CHAPTER 24

Jenna and Finn sat in the waiting room for what felt like an eternity. The staff had rushed his dog back to the surgical room and told him to wait out front. The vet finally returned an hour later, confirming that Eros had been stabbed, barely missing anything vital. They'd been able to repair the damage and stitched the pup up. Eros would have to stay at the clinic for several days, but barring complications, he'd fully recover. Finn broke down, his emotions spilling from relief.

Back in the car, Jenna couldn't contain her guilt. "Finn, I think you should take me home."

Finn jerked the car to the side of the road, horns blaring behind him as he did.

"What the fuck, Jenna. Why would I take you home?"

Jenna looked down at her hands, still stained with Eros's blood. She'd washed them at the vet's office, but there was still evidence of what happened.

"It's my fault Eros was hurt. He wouldn't have been nearly killed if I hadn't been with you. Someone followed me to your house. I couldn't live with myself if he'd died, Finn."

"You listen to me." Finn turned to look at her. "This is not your fault. Someone meant to hurt you, and Eros probably got in their way. He's not dead. And there is no way I am taking you home. I told you earlier that you're mine. I will not let some psychopath ruin your life, Jenna."

Finn kept her hand in his as he pulled back onto the road. Jenna didn't speak. She couldn't stop the tears from pouring out of her. This man had barreled his way into her life, and it scared her to think she was the reason he could be hurt, but it frightened her more to think of her life without him—she didn't know what that meant.

Did he feel the same for her?

—————

WHEN THEY NEARED Finn's house, she wasn't shocked to see a swarm of police cars parked in the driveway and on the street. Finn pulled alongside a patrol car and cut the engine.

"Jenna, I mean it when I say I'll protect you. I will not let someone torment you."

"Thank you, Finn."

"It's my job, Jenna."

He pushed the door open and slid out of his seat, leaving her alone in the car. His words punched her in the gut, reminding her that, while he was attracted to her, she was just a job to him. Jenna tried to rein in her feelings, sucking down the need to cry, and pushed herself to get out of the car. She would let him protect her, but she would need to protect her heart.

She was falling for Finn, but she wasn't so sure he felt the same, and she couldn't risk being hurt again—this time, her heart was at stake.

She approached Finn and Captain Hutchens as they spoke to Detective Peterson. Jenna could tell the men were tense. Finn's rigid body spoke of the anger he held.

"Miss Hardy," Detective Peterson greeted her with a cautious smile. "How are you doing?"

"Fine," her words clipped as she glanced at the men before her. She tried to avoid eye contact with Finn, her heart still bruised from his reminder that she was just a job.

The men shared a glance. Captain Hutchens cleared his throat, "We are going to place a marked unit outside tonight as a precaution."

"Ok." Jenna walked past the men. "I need to go wash up. Can I go inside?"

"Yeah, there was no evidence anyone went inside." Detective Peterson confirmed.

"Thanks. For everything."

The men watched as Jenna stormed up the steps and closed the door behind her. "What the fuck did you do to make her so pissed, Finn?" Hutchens cocked an eyebrow at him.

"Yeah—she was seriously frosty." Peterson chuckled. "You say something in the car to set her off?"

Finn thought back to their conversation. "Shit." He ran his palm over his face. "I think she misunderstood something I said."

"What the hell could she have misunderstood to piss her off?"

"I told her I wouldn't let some psychopath torment her. When she thanked me, I told her it was my job."

"Whoops." Peterson shook his head. "So, now she thinks you're only doing this because it's your job? Doesn't she know this isn't in a sergeant's job description?"

"Fuck." Finn glanced towards the house. "I need to talk to her."

"Yeah. You do. Go on, I'll let the uniform know he's staying parked outside tonight. See you tomorrow on shift, Judson."

Finn shook their hands and rushed up the steps. He locked up the house, made a quick call to check on Eros, and then headed upstairs. As soon as he stepped into his room, he heard the shower running. Quickly stripping his clothes, he opened the bathroom door and snuck inside. He watched her through the glass door as the water washed over her body.

Her back was to him, but he could tell she was crying. The way her shoulders were bunched and her hands clasped in front of her told him she was trying to hide the soft sobs coming from her. Tugging the door open, he slipped into the warm fog behind her.

CHAPTER 25

Jenna couldn't stop the tears or the feeling of her heart-shattering. In the last few days, she'd fallen in love with Finn. And hearing him say she was his job crushed her. Maybe she was overreacting, but he'd given no sign she was more than an attraction. Sure, the sex was unbelievable, but perhaps that's all it was for him. He'd said she was his, but maybe that'd only meant she was his job. She didn't know, but she felt trapped.

Trapped in gut-wrenching *sorrow*.

Trapped in *fear*.

There was nothing to stop the sobs spilling from her body. She was thankful the shower drowned out her cries.

She was startled when strong arms wrapped around her, pulling her against the solid wall of muscle she knew instantly was Finn.

Finn turned her to face him. "Look at me, sweetheart." Jenna shook her head, burying her face in his chest. He slipped his fingers beneath her chin, lifting her head to look at him. "I need to clear something up with you."

Jenna turned her head, looking towards the wall, too embarrassed to look at him fully.

"You misunderstood something, I said."

"I get it, Finn. You don't need to apologize. I'm just a job to you. You feel responsible for me."

Finn sighed. "You think this is my job? No, it's not. I work patrol, Jenna. Protecting you off duty is not part of my job description."

Jenna jerked toward him, her eyes locking onto his. "But you said…"

"I know what I said—but it's not what I meant… not like that. It's my job to protect you, yes. But it's not my job to guard you—keep you close to me. Having you here," he pressed his erection against her, "like this is not part of that either."

"It's just sex, Finn. Sex I started."

"Just sex? Is that what you think?" Finn backed her against the tile. "This is more than just sex, Jenna." He dipped his head, pressing his hot lips against her neck. "I told you you're mine. I meant that." He nipped her flesh. "And I didn't mean mine as in a job." He slipped his finger between her folds, pressing against her clit.

Jenna moaned, arching her back to press into him for more. "I meant you're mine to worship, Jenna. I don't want you here just to keep you safe." He curled his finger, slipping in another as he pumped his hand. Her pussy flooded with wetness, covering his fingers in her desire. "I want you here because I've fallen for you. Do you understand now?"

Jenna nodded against him, her orgasm bursting from her core as her pussy contracted around his digits. She screamed out his name, her head dropping against his shoulder as he took her in his arms. He turned off the water and lifted her against him.

His hands clasped around her ass as he walked her to the bed and dropped her to the mattress, both still soaking wet. He pushed her knees apart and dropped at the foot of the bed. Jenna propped herself on her elbows and started to speak, but Finn buried his face between her legs and licked. Her head dropped back, a moan filtering through the room.

She pushed her pussy into his face, giving him access to devour her honey. Finn dragged his tongue from the bottom of her cunt to the swollen bundle of nerves begging for attention. He sucked on her clit, gently biting down. The pressure sent a jolt of fire through her body, causing her to scream out. She writhed beneath him as he assaulted her clit like he was a madman. "Please… Oh God… Finn… I need you inside me… please." She pleaded, frantically tugging at his hair. Her body was on the verge of exploding.

Finn lifted his head, giving her a smoldering smile. "You want me to fuck you, Jenna?"

"Oh God—yes… *Please.*"

Finn shifted to his knees between her legs. Her slit was soaking wet and ready for him. He fisted his cock, sliding his hand up and down along his shaft.

"You want this, baby?" Jenna watched as he jerked himself in front of her. Biting her lip, she nodded. "Tell me what you want, Jenna."

"I want you to fill me up with your cock, Finn. Then I want you to make me scream as I come around you." She spread her legs wider.

Finn pressed his thumb to her clit, pinching it as he ran the head of his cock through her slit. Leaning over her, he pushed his crown between her lips and eased himself inside her. Jenna let out a hiss, her legs going around his waist. Finn began moving slowly, dipping in and pulling out, his eyes never straying from the sight of his dick disappearing between her folds.

He lifted his head, squeezing his eyes shut in ecstasy. "God-damn, Jenna." He pumped his hips harder. Jenna wiggled against him.

"Please… Fuck me harder, Finn."

Finn snapped, his hips hammering into hers. He leaned up, gripping her hips as he leaned back on his heels. Tugging her legs into a v, he angled her body so he could press deeper. Jenna screamed out, her hands cupping her breasts.

"That's it, baby. Squeeze your nipples for me." Jenna watched as molten desire filled Finn's eyes as she pinched her pert tips between her fingers. He dropped her legs, covering her body with his. Finn grabbed her hips and drove his dick into her hard.

"Goddamn…" He clenched his eyes, grinding his teeth, "Come with me, baby…"

Jenna gripped his shoulders, tilting her head back as her stomach tightened. Her body gave in, her orgasm taking over.

"FINN!… OH GOD!" she screamed, clenching hard on his cock.

The room spun as Finn pounded into her. She could feel him swell inside her, his seed bursting out of him with such force she could swear she felt it deep in her chest.

"FUCK!" He let out a guttural cry.

His body jerked against hers. His breathing was ragged as he collapsed next to her in the bed.

She snuggled against him, lost for words. There was no way she could explain what just happened. Jenna knew what they'd just shared was more than sex—Finn had just obliterated any barriers between them.

"Woman. You're mine. And if that didn't brand you, I don't know what will." Finn kissed her head. He lay there for another minute before getting up and grabbing a towel. He gently cleaned her off, then pulled the blanket over her naked form. Grabbing his boxers, he slipped them on. "I'm going to go make us something to eat. Be back in a few." He kissed her head. As he walked out the door, Finn turned to her. "Jenna?"

Jenna glanced at him. "Yeah?"

"I know you might not be ready to hear this—but I love you." He stepped out, pulling the door shut.

CHAPTER 26

JENNA DIDN'T SAY ANYTHING WHEN FINN RETURNED WITH soup and sandwiches. She wasn't sure she was ready to admit her feelings out loud just yet—even though she was pretty sure she loved him, too.

Instead, they ate dinner and talked about their families. Finn told her about how his parents were disappointed he'd been divorced and his choice of profession. Jenna was shocked to learn he was rich but didn't use his family money for anything. He wanted to make his way in life–which she found admirable. Like her, he was an only child. Jenna shared how she'd wanted a large family but how Alec had refused. Finn told her he'd wanted a lot of kids, too, but Marley, his ex-wife, had kept that from happening by going behind his back and getting an IUD.

"So, it sounds like we share a lot in common." Jenna smiled and snuggled against him in the bed. They'd stayed there most of the evening, only getting out to use the bathroom or return the plates to the kitchen. "Well, except you don't have a psycho ex trying to kill you."

Finn kissed Jenna. "He won't touch you, Jenna. I mean it. If it is Alec doing all this, he won't get away with it."

"I just wish we knew where he was."

"We'll find him. Between Peterson and his parole officer, they'll weed him out."

Jenna shifted her body. "I wonder how long Becky and Mr. Harlow have been together. That was weird, right?" Jenna giggled, remembering her friend's expression when they'd busted in on their heated embrace.

"You should call her." Finn grabbed his phone and handed it to Jenna. "Use mine. I left yours downstairs."

Jenna smiled, propping herself up on his chest. She found Becky's contact and pressed the call button. It was after ten o'clock, but she knew Becky was still awake.

"Finn? Is everything alright?" Becky sounded panicked.

"It's Jenna. I'm fine."

"Jenna… thank God. I was worried he was calling to tell me something else happened."

Jenna launched into the day's events, catching Becky up on the ever-growing mystery of her stalker. "That's fucked up. Is Eros ok?" Becky asked. "I know that dog is like his damn kid —he was all Finn had after that bitch left him."

Jenna hid the guilt she was feeling. "Yeah. Vet says he will make a full recovery. We can bring him home in a couple of days."

"Bring him home? Jenna sounds like you're getting comfortable over there."

"You know what I mean. Besides, you seemed mighty comfortable in your classroom today."

"Oh—um…" Jenna could hear Becky shifting. The sound of a man's voice was muffled in the background.

"OH, my GOD. You're not alone, are you?"

Becky giggled, "No. Well… look. We've been seeing each other for a while—but him being the boss, we had to keep it on the down low. You can't tell anyone, Jenna. He could get fired."

"Who the hell am I going to tell? You're my only friend in the building, Becky. I can't believe you and Mr. Harlow."

"David." Becky corrected her, "Please call him David. Hearing Mr. Harlow is weird."

"Is it serious?"

"Yeah… I think so. Hell, we're together just about every night, Jenna."

"Well, I won't keep you. I just wanted to check in and let you know I was alive."

"I figured you were too busy getting it on with that hunk of a man in bed with you."

"What? How did you know he was in bed with me?" Jenna glanced down at Finn, who was listening to their call.

"Please, you're using his phone, Jenna."

"Oh, right."

"Tell Finn hello. I'll call you tomorrow." Becky giggled, "I gotta go." Jenna could hear someone talking to her.

"Fine… tell David hello for me as well."

Jenna disconnected the call, stretching across Finn's body to put his phone on the table. As she did, he caught her nipple in his mouth.

Jenna moaned at the sensation of his warm lips on her. She wiggled against him. "You're insatiable."

"Can you blame me?" He mumbled against her skin. Jenna smiled, leaning up on her knees as she straddled him.

"I think I know how to make you sleepy." She sank herself onto his hard cock, her eyes closing as he filled her up.

"Fuck." Finn groaned as she moved against him. He couldn't take his eyes off her as she rocked against him. "Goddamn… Jenna, I'm not going to last long this time. *Christ.*" He bucked his hips against her as she rode him hard.

Fortunately for him, she didn't take long to reach her climax. She spasmed around his cock, milking him dry as his release washed over him. Jenna collapsed against him, snuggling her body against his as he turned off the light, pulling the covers over them.

Jenna twirled her fingers against his muscular chest, listening as his breaths evened out. Stealing a glance at his face, she smiled to see him sleeping.

Burrowing into his hold, Jenna sighed. "I love you, Finn." She whispered into the darkness.

Soon, she'd be brave enough to tell him when he was awake.

CHAPTER 27

Finn stretched and felt Jenna move against him.

"Morning." She smiled. "Sleep well?"

"Yeah, how about you?"

"Better than I have in a long time." Jenna glanced up at him. "What time is it?"

"Almost eleven. I need to get up and get ready for work."

"Oh…" Jenna tried to hide her disappointment.

"I'll come back once I go on duty. Captain won't care if I hang out here if I'm listening out to the radio. Perks of being a sergeant and living in the city limits." Finn grinned at her, pressing his lips to hers as he slipped out of the bed.

"Can I use your car to go to the grocery store?" Finn hesitated, staring at her as if he wasn't sure how to respond. "I'll be careful, Finn. There and then straight home. I wanted to make dinner tonight, and there isn't much in your fridge."

"Well, you'll have to drop me off at the station, but as long as you promise to come straight home after, you can use my car."

"Thanks. I'll jump in the shower after you."

"Or you could just take one with me."

Jenna giggled, "We know how that will turn out. No, go ahead. I'm going to check my work email and grab some clothes." Jenna stood, the covers pooling at her feet.

Finn's eyes darkened with desire. "Fuck, you make it hard to get in the shower." He stalked towards her and scooped her up. Tossing her over his shoulder, he smacked her ass. "I don't care if I'm late. You're getting in the shower with me."

<hr>

AFTER A VIGOROUS ROUND in the shower, Jenna finally dropped Finn off at the station. She watched as he disappeared behind the glass doors before driving off. As soon as she parked, she reached for her wallet inside her bag, only to find it wasn't there.

"Shit," she muttered into the empty car. Closing her eyes, she remembered the last place she had her purse was at the school. It must have fallen out when she was packing up her classroom.

Putting the car in reverse, she pulled out of the parking lot and headed towards the school. Pulling her phone out, she dialed Finn. She'd promised to go to the store and straight home, but grocery shopping was a bust without her wallet. After leaving him a quick message that she was running to the school to retrieve her wallet, she parked the car and scanned the parking lot. It wasn't a surprise to see only a handful of vehicles. Most everyone was gone, leaving only maintenance and administration in the building.

Jenna grabbed her badge and headed towards the side entrance closest to her classroom. Scanning her way in, she hurried to her room. She glanced into the darkened classroom, spying her wallet exactly where she'd expected it to be, and scooped it up. Turning to leave, she was startled to find she wasn't alone.

"Alec." She sucked in a breath.

"Hello, Jenna. Long time no see."

CHAPTER 28

"Hey, Sarge." Grimes walked into the briefing room. Hutchens had called a meeting with the shift to review some new information about Alec Brown—Jenna's ex-husband.

"Grimes, how's it going?" Finn smiled at his team member.

"Heard Peterson has some sort of news about your girl."

"Hope it's telling us they found the prick of an ex-husband," muttered Hall, one of the guys on his shift, as he followed Grimes in.

"Alright, boys," Hutchens and Peterson stepped into the room. "We have evidence that proves Alec is, in fact, Jenna Hardy's stalker. An eyewitness places him in town, making him our prime suspect."

Captain handed everyone a photo of her ex. "This is our guy. I want everyone on alert. He's already gone after her multiple times, including injuring Judson's dog."

Everyone nodded, mumbling the same thing. They all wanted to catch the bastard. Finn glanced down at his phone, noticing a missed call from Jenna. Seeing he had a message from her, he quickly listened.

"Hey, Finn. I know I promised to go to the store and go straight home, but I realized my wallet must have fallen out of my purse yesterday. I am going to run over to the school and check my room. No worries, I'll be quick. Call you in a few."

Finn sucked in a breath, his gut churning with trepidation. He tapped the call button and pressed the phone to his ear. Jenna's voicemail picked up immediately.

"Hey, Jenna, it's Finn. Call me when you get this message."

Hutchens glanced over at him. "Problem, Judson?"

"I don't know, sir—just a feeling. Jenna left me a message that she was running by the school to get her wallet. She's not answering her phone."

"Call again." the Captain ordered as he came to stand beside Finn, looking as nervous as he felt. He redialed her number.

"Nothing. Still got her voice mail. I'll ride by the school."

"I'll follow you."

Grimes darted back into the room as the two of them headed out the door. "Hey, Sarge. Dispatch just got a Signal 69—person armed call. It was from one of the maintenance men at the school. He told dispatch a strange guy was hanging around the building. When he went to ask the guy what he was doing there, the maintenance man saw a gun in the dude's waist band, so he called us instead."

"FUCK!" Finn shoved past Grimes, bolting out the door. "Get some units over there. It's him, Captain. Goddamn it! Jenna's at the school."

The three men ran towards their cars, Finn beating them out of the parking lot and tearing off down the road. He kept trying to call Jenna, getting increasingly angry when it continued to go to voicemail. Tossing his phone to the seat beside him, he closed his eyes and prayed Jenna was safe.

"ALEC. YOU SHOULDN'T BE HERE."

"What? You think a little piece of paper would keep me from you?" Alec stalked toward her.

"Stop. Don't come near me." Jenna put her hand up, backing away from him.

"I saw you with him, Jenna. Did you tell him you belonged to me? Does he know you married me... making you my property?"

"I am no one's property, Alec. Not yours, not his." Jenna bumped into a desk, causing her to fall backward, her butt hitting the smooth surface.

"You're wrong, Jenna. You'll always belong to me."

"Fuck you, Alec."

She saw it coming. His hand moved in slow motion as he backhanded her, tossing her to the floor. He snatched her by her hair, dragging her onto her knees.

"Don't make me do this, Jenna. Why can't you do what you're told? Fuck!" Alec bellowed, pulling at his hair as he looked down at her. "Get UP!" He shoved his knee into her back, causing her to fall forward onto her hands.

"Alec… please… stop."

"NO! Get up… NOW!" Jenna climbed to her feet, turning to look at the monster she once thought she loved. Looking at him now, she realized what she'd felt for him had never been confirmed, unlike what she felt for Finn. Thinking of him made her suck in a sob.

"Please… Alec."

"That's right, Jenna. Beg for me."

CHAPTER 29

Finn had never felt so much rage. He and Grimes had beaten everyone on the scene and opted to enter the building. Seeing his car in the parking lot, he knew Jenna could be in trouble, and he wasn't waiting. They'd cleared the first two hallways, ensuring they were empty. Now, heading down Jenna's hall, he and Grimes paused when they heard a man's voice, followed by Jenna's cry.

Grimes gripped Finn's shoulder, stopping him from barging into the room. "We need to do this right. Storming in there could get her killed," Grimes whispered behind Finn.

Finn nodded. Grimes was right. As much as he wanted to storm into the room, he didn't want to risk Jenna's safety. He knew Alec had a gun, making the situation even more volatile.

Finn listened as Alec taunted Jenna. It was killing him to stand by and do nothing. He nearly came unhinged when he heard Jenna cry out in pain. Grimes bristled behind him. Thankfully, their radios were fed into an earpiece, making it silent for anyone beside them. Hutchens had confirmed they were outside the backdoor to her classroom, ready to pounce if Alec tried to leave through that exit.

Finn could hear Jenna pleading with him, begging him to leave, but Alec would not let her out of his clutches again. He believed Jenna was his.

JENNA WISHED she'd listened to Finn and just stayed home. But standing there in front of Alec, she knew this moment was inevitable—Alex would have gotten to her, eventually. He was delusional into believing she was his.

"Alec, you need help. Please, let me get you some help."

"NO!" He screamed, slamming his hands into the desk beside her. "I just need you. When we leave here together, you'll see. You were meant to be with me, Jenna."

"If that were true, Alec… why do you hurt me?"

"What? That's your fault. You make me do it. I must teach you a lesson, Jenna. Make you understand I'm in control."

Jenna nodded, "You're right, Alec. It's my fault."

Jenna swallowed the bile rising in her throat. Maybe if she convinced him she believed him, he wouldn't kill her. She spotted something metal in the corner and realized maintenance had left some of the piping they were using to replace the older ones. It was propped against the wall. Jenna eased her way toward it, her eyes never straying from his. "Alec, let's just leave here together. OK? We can go somewhere and fix this… fix us." She flattened against the wall, sliding her hands around the cool metal as Alec stalked toward her.

"Don't lie to me, Jenna."

"I'm not lying." She gripped the pipe tighter.

"What about the guy you were fucking last night? Huh? I saw you with him, Jenna."

"What? How…" Jenna closed her eyes. That meant he'd been in the house with them.

"After I took care of that damn dog, it was much easier to get into the house."

Jenna gasped. She couldn't believe Alec had confessed to hurting Eros. "Why, Alec. Why'd you stab the dog?"

"That fucker tried to bite me when I snuck into the backyard. Had to keep from losing a limb. Fucker was heavy to drag around to the front, too." Alec sneered, his face contorting with rage. "You fucking care about that cop, don't you? I'll take care of that pig—he can't have you, Jenna."

"Please, Alec." Jenna shifted her body just as Alec stepped in front of her. She held firm to the pipe, praying her plan worked she leapt forward. Using the adrenaline coursing through her body, Jenna brought the metal up and struck his head. Blood splattered across her face as Alec crumpled to the floor. Jenna let out a gut-wrenching scream as she collapsed onto the floor.

CHAPTER 30

Finn's heart stopped when he heard Jenna scream. He didn't care about anything but getting to her and burst into the classroom. He rushed to her side when he saw her crumpled on the floor, covered in blood—the sight nearly did him in. He could vaguely hear Grimes talking in his ear, calling for an ambulance and a supervisor. Finn pulled Jenna into his arms and searched her for injuries and saw that the blood wasn't hers. He pressed her body to his chest. "Baby, please wake up. Jenna… can you hear me?"

Jenna stirred in his arms, "Finn…" she moaned, blinking her eyes open. "OH MY GOD, Alec… Finn," She jerked against him.

"It's ok, Jenna. You're safe."

Jenna saw Alec on the ground, his expression hollow as he stared at her with vacant eyes. "I killed him… Finn, I killed him." A sob tore from her lips.

Finn pressed her to his chest, "It's ok, baby. He was going to kill you. You're safe now."

She cried against him, locked in his embrace as the room filled with a flurry of activity. Captain Hutchens tapped Finn on the shoulder. "Judson, take her outside and let EMS check her over. We'll need her to give a statement down at the station."

"Got it." Finn stood, cradling her in his arms, and carried her from the room. He sat down on the back of the ambulance, giving EMS room to check her over. Once he got a clean bill of health, he scooped her up and carried her to his patrol car.

Finn set her down in the passenger seat and squatted between her knees. "I'm going to grab a shirt from my bag. Wait here." Jenna nodded, clearly still in shock at the events. "Alright, baby. I'm going to help you change. Ok? Can you lift your arms?" Finn didn't care that they were in the middle of the parking lot with people milling around. He needed to get her out of the bloody shirt. Jenna lifted her arms, giving him room to pull the top over her head. He eased his shirt over her head, gliding it down her arms. Using the blood-stained blouse, he wiped the evidence of what happened from her cheeks and forehead. "Alright, let me get you buckled in."

Finn strapped her in and shut the door. He held her hand as he drove her to the station to meet Detective Peterson. Finn knew giving her a statement would be hard, but he'd be beside her when she did.

JENNA DIDN'T REMEMBER the drive to the station. She only remembered the vacant look in Alec's eyes as he fell to the ground. She hadn't meant to kill him. She just wanted to get away from him. Jenna knew she should feel some remorse for ending a person's life, but all she felt was relief.

"Alright, baby. We're here." Jenna glanced at Finn, realizing they'd parked in front of the station. He hopped out, came to her side, and opened the door. Holding his hand out, he helped Jenna stand. "You alright?"

"Yeah." Jenna nodded, shutting the door behind her.

"We need to meet with Detective Peterson. He needs to get your statement."

"Ok."

"Jenna, I'll be right there with you."

She nodded, following Finn as he held her hand in his. The interview went faster than she expected, Peterson assuring her it was self-defense and that there was nothing to worry about. Alec had violated a bunch of laws, making it well within her rights to defend herself the way she had. Peterson told her they'd found his car a few blocks from the school and that Alec had plenty of evidence inside indicating he'd planned to kill her. Jenna shuddered, thinking that today could have been her last.

Captain Hutchens told Finn to take a few days off and take care of her. Jenna was grateful for everyone's involvement in ending the case. Someone had brought Finn's car to the station, allowing him to drive them home.

Becky was at Finn's house waiting when they pulled into the driveway. She rushed to Jenna, helping her out of the car before wrapping her arms around Jenna, both girls crying in each other's embrace.

Finn helped Jenna up the steps, Becky holding onto one side of her. Once inside, Jenna told them she just wanted to shower. Becky nodded and helped Jenna up the stairs. Finn watched as they disappeared into his room. Finally letting out the breath he'd been holding, he sat down. He wanted to comfort her but knew her friend needed to do this. Becky had been just as worried as everyone else, so seeing her like this probably gutted her, too.

"Hey, Finn," Becky said as she descended the stairs. "She asked to be left alone. I told her to call me tomorrow, but will you let me know if she needs anything?" Becky's eyes were wet with tears. Finn reached out and pulled his friend into a hug.

"Thank you for being her friend. I'll call you later. Let you know how she's doing."

"Thanks." Becky pulled free, "Finn?"

"Yeah?"

"Take care of her. She deserves something good for once."

Finn walked her to the door. "Don't worry, Becky. I'm not going anywhere." He smiled.

"You love her," Becky said matter of fact.

"Yeah—I do." He smiled as she got in her car and waved. Shutting the door, he headed up the stairs to check on Jenna. He would do whatever it took to make her happy again.

She was it for him.

He hoped she felt the same, but if not, he'd wait until she did. He wasn't walking away from this woman.

CHAPTER 31

Jenna watched as the water ran red from her body. Alec's blood covered her arms and skin. Scrubbing until her skin was raw, Jenna let the tears run wild. She couldn't control the sobs wracking her body. Collapsing, Jenna drew her legs to her chest and cried. She'd killed a man. A man that had nearly cost her life, yet she still felt dirty.

"Jenna," Finn's voice cut through the steam as he opened the shower door.

His arms held her as he scooped her off the shower floor. Finn pressed her to his chest, his shirt soaking through as he turned off the faucet. Grabbing a towel, he wrapped her as best he could and carried her to the bed. Pulling the covers back, he sat her down, running the towel over her body to dry her skin. Toweling her hair dry, he tossed the wet cotton to the floor. He laid her back, slipping her feet beneath the cool sheets. Stripping off his shirt and pants, he dropped beside her on the bed. Pulling her body into his arms, he wrapped her in his embrace.

"Let it out, baby. I got you."

Jenna cried as Finn held her. He stroked her hair, pressing kisses to her head as she let the day wash over her. Finn listened as she let her emotions work themselves out. He cradled her tighter, silently telling her he was there for her. Finally, after what felt like hours, Jenna fell asleep.

Finn climbed from the bed, glancing at her petite frame before leaving the room. He wanted to order food to ensure she ate something, and he needed to check on Eros. He'd only been downstairs long enough to call the vet when he heard her scream.

Bolting up the steps, he rushed to the bedside. Jenna was screaming out in her sleep.

"Baby, I got you." He pressed kisses to her head, slipping beside her again, and pulled her into his arms. "Shhh, Jenna, you're safe." He rocked her until he felt her relax against him.

He sat up against the headboard, running his fingers through her hair. Once he was sure she was asleep again, he slipped out and grabbed his phone. Hurrying back to the bed, he called Becky. He asked her to bring some dinner, explaining what happened and how he was afraid to leave her side. Becky didn't hesitate. She offered to stay the night, giving him an extra set of hands so he could stay with her, but Finn told her they'd be alright if she could just something to eat.

Becky made it to the house faster than he'd expected. Finn thanked her and set the soup she'd brought by the bed. Becky excused herself, telling him to call her if he needed her again. Once she pulled the door closed, Finn woke Jenna.

"Jenna," he pressed a kiss to her cheek. "Baby, can you wake up and eat something?"

Jenna cracked her eyes open. "Finn?"

"Yeah—can you sit up?"

Jenna nodded and pushed herself up, the sheet slipping down her nude chest. "Where are my clothes?"

"You kinda lost it in the shower. I got you out and put you to bed. Hang on." Finn hopped out and grabbed one of his t-shirts. "Here, let me help you put this on." Finn slipped the cotton tee over her head and situated the blanket back over her thighs. "Becky brought some soup. Can you try to eat for me?"

"What time is it?"

"Almost nine." Finn set a tray on her lap; the scent of noodle soup filled her nostrils.

"Smells good." She smiled, grabbed the spoon, and shoved it in her mouth. Finn watched as she emptied the bowl. "I guess I was hungry." She gave him a half smile.

"You want to talk about what happened?" Finn asked hesitantly.

Jenna closed her eyes. "No, but I probably should. The one thing my therapist told me after I left Alec the first time was that hiding behind the trauma only made it worse." Jenna swallowed, trying to gather her thoughts. Finn grabbed her hand, lacing his fingers with hers.

"Take your time." Jenna opened her eyes and looked into his deep green irises. She told him what happened, from the moment she turned and found Alec standing in her room to the decision to hit him. Once she'd finished telling her story, Jenna felt a weight lift off her shoulders. Finn tugged her into his arms, pressing his lips on her skin. "You're safe now, Jenna."

She sighed into his arms. "I guess that means I can go home."

Finn tensed around her. "Um… yeah, I guess it does."

Jenna took a breath. "Finn," she whispered against his chest. "I don't want to leave."

Finn relaxed, relief washing over him. "I don't want you to either." He leaned back to meet her gaze. "I know it's fast, but move in with me. Stay here."

Jenna smiled, leaning up to press her lips against his. "Ok."

Finn laid her back, kissing the skin along her neck. His hands fumbled with the shirt, slipping beneath the hem and cupping her breasts. Jenna leaned up, tugging it over her head and tossing it to the floor.

She pressed her lips to his, winding her fingers into his hair. Finn slid between her legs, worshiping her body with each kiss. Jenna and Finn lost themselves in each other, taking time to explore one another, until finally, he drove himself inside her. Jenna cried out, her hips rising to match his thrusts. Finn's hands roamed her body as he savored every gasp she gave him.

"That's it, baby. I'm close. You going to come with me? Fuck my dick, Jenna."

Jenna wrapped her legs around his waist, pulling him deeper inside her as she ground her clit against his shaft. "I'm…

Oh…Oh… FINN!" she screamed out, her walls clamping down on his cock.

Finn let out a guttural sound as he emptied his seed inside her. His semen staining her walls.

Pressing a kiss to her neck, he whispered, "I will never get tired of hearing you call out my name."

"That's good because I love calling out your name."

Finn smiled against her skin. "I love you, Jenna."

"I love you, too, Finn."

He closed his eyes as she snuggled against him under the covers. He'd never let this woman go. She had burrowed her way into his heart and took root. Finn would spend the rest of his life showing Jenna how special she was. His heart belonged to her.

CHAPTER 32

Jenna dug her toes in the sand, staring over the ocean. It's been almost two months since Alec tormented her, and she took his life. Glancing over at Becky, who was lounging on a chair beside her, Jenna asked her friend, "Where did the guys go again?"

"To get some food or something. You know men, they're always hungry for food or sex." Becky laughed.

They'd brought their men along for their summer vacation. It was supposed to be a staycation, but Finn decided to spring for an all-inclusive trip to Jamaica. Becky and Mr. Harlow—rather David—got engaged shortly after the incident. He resigned as principal, taking a position at the county office so they could be together.

Becky offered to transfer, but he felt like she needed to be there for Jenna. Jenna was forever grateful to him because as much as she told herself she'd be fine, she knew having Becky there would make the first day back easier.

Finn and she had gone back to her classroom a few weeks later, and Finn held her while she cried. Of course, the carpet had been replaced, leaving no evidence of the incident, but Jenna knew—and that was enough reminder for her.

"I can't believe we have to go back to work in a week. I could just live here." Becky moaned, stretching her feet in the sand.

"Me too… there is so much to do when I get back. The realtor told me everything was set for closing."

"Well, at least you already moved all your shit out."

"True."

Jenna smiled, remembering the day Finn and his buddies at the station helped her move out of her house. She was sad to say goodbye to the place that had helped her start over, but living with Finn was better than she could have imagined. Every day was better than the last. Even though they'd only been together a few months, Jenna felt like she'd known him for eternity.

"Here they come," Becky grinned, watching as David and Finn stalked toward them. Jenna loved seeing Finn's bare chest. His arms and chest were covered in tattoos, tracing the well-defined muscles he carried.

"Stop drooling, Jenna." Becky laughed at her, snapping her out of her lustful trance.

"I can't help it. Every time I see him, I want to fuck his brains out." Jenna turned back to her friend and gave her a cocky grin.

"Eeew… I did not need that visual—but I feel the same way looking at my man." Becky grinned.

"Ok… we're even. I don't want to visualize my ex-principal and you in the throes of passion." Jenna shuddered.

"Hey, baby." Finn leaned down and kissed her lips as he flopped beside her in the sand.

Jenna smiled, turning to see David dragging Becky to her feet. "Hey, where are you two going?"

"Um," Becky smiled, "David wants to show me something back in the room."

Jenna tossed her hand up. "I don't need to know. We will catch up to you guys later." She watched as Becky and David stumbled towards their room. "Bet I know what he wants to show her." Jenna waggled her eyebrows at Finn and couldn't stop laughing.

"Want to take a walk with me?" Finn stood, holding out his hand toward her.

"Sure," She stood, wrapping her arms around his neck. "I love you." She kissed his mouth as he pulled her against his chest.

"I love you, too. Come on, let's go before I fuck you right here on the beach." Jenna blushed, holding his hand as he tugged her down to the shoreline.

They walked silently, holding hands as the waves beat against the sand. "Everything alright, Finn?"

Finn stopped, glancing out across the blue water. "Everything is perfect." He turned to her, taking her hands in his. "Jenna, this has been the best week of my life. You've given me back a part of my heart I thought I'd lost. You crashed into my life like a tidal wave, dragging me back into the life of the living.

Before you, I just drifted. Work consumed me, and hook-ups always failed to fill the gaping hole in my chest."

He smiled, "You are the light in the dark. The wind that blows through the trees. The blood that pumps through my veins. I can't imagine a day without you in my life." Finn reached into his pocket and dropped to one knee. "Jenna Hardy, I love you with every fiber of my soul. Will you make me the happiest man in the world and become my wife?"

Jenna gasped, staring at the man who meant more than her breath, "Yes… Finn… Yes, I'll marry you."

Finn stood, pulling her into his arms. They kissed, pulling apart as Finn slipped the ring on her finger. "I love you, Jenna."

Jenna held onto him as he kissed her, the waves lapping at their ankles. Resting their foreheads together, Jenna couldn't hide her smile. This man had brought joy back into her life—he'd shown her love existed.

"I love you, Finn."

EPILOGUE

Jason Hunter stared at the invitation to his friend Finn's wedding. Everyone around him seemed to find their happy ending, except him. He tossed his empty cup into the trash just as the tones for a call blared through the speakers.

Signal 41—possible injuries. Truck versus motorcycle. Squad 6, Truck 6, and Medic 6 respond to 7th and Main.

Jason hurried out to the truck bay and tugged his turnout gear on. Climbing into the squad, his partner, Dawson Ford, hopped in the driver's seat. Henry Jones, aka Jonesy, a third man on the special operations unit, poured into the back seat just as Dawson rolled the truck out the front door.

"Maybe it won't be a bad one. Sometimes bikers just lay their bikes down in the dirt to avoid a car or truck," Henry called out from the back seat as they neared the scene.

"I hope so. I don't want to be stuck here all damn day." Dawson huffed as he pulled the truck to a stop. "But something tells me this will change someone's life."

Jason stared at his friend, his words twisting inside his chest more than usual. Anytime a motorcycle tangled with a car, the odds never favored the cycle's driver. And looking out the window, the scene told him this would not be quick. The motorcycle lay on its side, crumpled beneath the front end of a semi-truck. The rider was on his back a few feet from the crumpled metal twisted in a heap on the grass.

This call was going to change *everything*.

Sometimes, in the wake of tragedy, you find love…
Find out if this jaded fireman opens his heart again in
Signal 41: Saving Carson

ALSO BY LC TAYLOR

Simply scan the QR code to find your next great read.

Can't scan?

No worries… simply visit

https://www.flowcode.com/page/lctaylor.doripulitano

ABOUT THE AUTHOR

"Grab me a shot of whiskey. These books are about tattooed men and guns!"

What can I say? I'm a down home southern girl who bleeds red, white, and blue, so welcome to My world. I'm an International and USA Today best-selling author, who's an unapologetic down-home southern gal, with a bit of a dirty mouth.

But… I've never met a brooding hero I didn't love. I write my men cut, tattooed and tender, for their down, but-not-out ladies, who just need a little love from the right man.

When I'm not writing my Crossroads Heroes series, creating swoon-worthy love connections, or indulging my darker desires as my alter ego Dori P, I'm curled up with a glass of peach crown and my very own sexy tattooed cop on the couch watching reruns of Chicago Fire..

facebook.com/AuthorLCTaylor

instagram.com/authorlctaylor

bookbub.com/authors/lc-taylor

goodreads.com/authorlctaylor

tiktok.com/NerdyDirtyBookTok

youtube.com/NerdyDirtyBooks

x.com/NerdyDirtyBooks